Treasure in the Deep

TREASURE IN THE DEEP

Written by

Starr Green

First edition December 2022
Map design: Megan Scott
Cover design by: Earthy Info
Interior book design by: Earthy Info

ISBN 978-1-955561-46-4 (hardcover)
ISBN 978-1-955561-47-1 (softcover)
ISBN 978-1-955561-48-8 (ebook)

Library of Congress Control Number: 2022949759

Earthy Info
Portland, Oregon
www.earthyinfo.com

Pronunciation Guide

Fia — Fee-uh
Lugh — Loo
Manannán Mac Lir — Mon-ah-non Mac Leer
Sidhe Realm — She re-lm
Tua De Dannan — Two-ah Day Dan-on
Tua De (shortened) — Two-ah Day

CHAPTER 1

Piper

Picking up another small box, Piper escaped the chaos in the house by carrying the box to Wave Sweeper, the magical ship where she lived. It was parked in the grassy backyard, flat-bottomed but otherwise pirate-shaped with a dragon figurehead. A stack of belongings had accumulated next to the rope ladder. The shimmering blue and green sails hung slack in the windless summer heat of the American southwest.

A man appeared in the space next to her, his blueish-black hair gleaming in the blazing sun. Lucky, the god of travelers, was missing his usual tailored long coat. His vest was absent as well. Even his prim fitted button-up shirt was loose at the neck, with the sleeves rolled to his elbows. Similar to Piper, his pale skin was already pink, with the beginning of a sunburn.

He took the box from Piper, asking, "Are we leaving soon?"

"I hope so," Piper said while trying to edge into the meager shade the ship provided. Growing up on the southeast coast had not prepared her for heat that could melt roads. Her light brown side braid had become loose, and the strands stuck to her sweaty neck. Her lungs burned, and she wanted to return to Ireland as soon as possible. The island had become her adopted home and won her heart, along with the people she'd met there.

When Lucky bent to pick up the box she'd brought, Piper noticed he'd also abandoned his shoes and socks. She was often barefoot, like now, but had never seen her impeccably dressed friend without his sturdy yet stylish, boots.

"Are they still arguing?" Lucky asked. Piper nodded, then laughed as Lucky rolled his vivid green eyes. "I suppose that wedded bliss also awaits us?"

Piper wrinkled her nose. "Not me. I'm not getting married to MacLir or anyone. Do you think Brigit will marry you?"

"Never say never." Lucky winked and disappeared with a slight pop.

Shaking her head, Piper hesitantly moved back toward the house. She'd recently created a baby with the man she loved but wasn't thinking about marriage at eighteen. The pair had enjoyed a few quiet months together with the infant, despite the unrest in the magical community. However, she had an uneasy feeling that life with the god of the sea might always be hectic—something her upbringing as a sheltered autistic child had not prepared her for. She felt stronger these days than her age would suggest, more confident in her instincts and slightly better able to speak her mind. However, conflict still made her edgy.

As she got to the front door, she could hear them again. They weren't yelling, but from the tone drifting down from upstairs, it was clear the conversation between Clara and her husband was not happy. Clara was leaving. She'd secretly packed everything she wanted to take, then called Piper.

When they arrived, Clara met them at the door and thanked them for coming quickly. Then, after explaining that her twins had left for college several days before, she'd added, "These days, I feel like my husband and I are so unbearably different."

Piper wondered if she'd ever feel that way about MacLir. At the moment, they were surprisingly similar. Acting young and silly for their ages. United in their love for each other and their new daughter, Emily.

Maybe Clara needed a new romance in her life. To rediscover how fun it could be. Piper had decided to discreetly use her powers while Clara explained to Lucky what needed loading. After getting together with MacLir, she'd been made a goddess of love, something she was finally getting used to almost a year later. Activating her power away from Ireland was a little more tiring, pulling power from any bits of wild nature around her, but it still worked.

Glancing sideways at Clara, she stared for a moment, then felt the mental pictures arriving. Piper looked down at her hands, so no one noticed her glazed eyes. Usually, she saw the beginnings of a romance and where it might lead in the visions. This time... nothing. In her mind's eye, Clara stood on the deck of Wave Sweeper. The sunset lit up the warm brown tones of her skin while the wind blew softly through her rich curly brunette hair. And she was smiling. Then the vision faded.

Nothing. No future romance? It was rare, and Piper was always vaguely unsettled when it happened. Wasn't there someone for everyone? It was telling that Piper didn't see the past when Clara had met her current husband. That meant they weren't right for each other to start with.

Sad that Clara had nothing to look forward to, Piper was glad the older autistic woman would be away from a place that made her unhappy. Although, she thought the getaway was not happening quickly enough.

Pausing in the doorway again, she considered interrupting and insisting it was time to go. Clara's husband was not violent, though, so the woman would come out when she was ready. After grabbing all the last items from the house in one load, Piper deposited them in the dead grass next to the ship and climbed the rope ladder.

Clara

Clara was tired.

Tired of cooking badly for four people and hearing the complaints about it.

Tired of picking up socks off the carpet she could never keep clean.

Tired of this argument and all the similar ones before it.

"I'm tired of being tired," she said to the man she thought she loved.

"Well, you never smile anymore," he replied, finally calming a little to see her side of things.

Actually, she couldn't remember the last time she'd smiled. No, wait, that wasn't true. She'd smiled during a dinner party at her sister's home in Ireland. During dessert, Piper and her love were acting like newlyweds with their public display of affection. The whole thing had ended in an endearing food fight between the two, and she'd had to smile.

Although, was that really months ago? She hadn't smiled in months? Worse, how long before that? Or, more importantly, when was the last time she'd been happy at home? When the twins were young, she decided. Maybe around the time they were in kindergarten. Then everything had gone… not wrong, but not right either.

She squished the fur of the horse plushie in her arms and watched it bounce back as she considered why she was leaving. In trying to maintain a chaotic household, she'd lost sight of everything she liked about herself. Her hobbies were pushed aside, and her personality was smothered in her duties as a wife and mother. So in deciding to leave now, she felt like she was taking back her life.

She'd move close to Amy and calmly start being the fun aunt and nothing more to anyone. "Good Gravy! Enough. I'm leaving. We have children together, so you'll see me again sometime. There will be graduations, weddings, baby namings, and grandkids to fawn over together. So... I'll see you later."

Clara walked out of the room and out of the house, careful not to bump any doors in case they slammed. She wasn't angry, only ready to move on. Seeing her luggage and boxes gone, she proceeded to the ship. Hugging her plushie tight as she climbed the rope ladder. When she reached the deck, Wave Sweeper rose in the air.

The big white farmhouse in front of her faded, melting and blurring into the distance until it all disappeared, replaced with a field of prairie grass. Once Piper had explained that longer trips were easier in the parallel realm where gods and faeries lived. The Otherworld, they called it. A pristine wilderness compared to the settled land in the human realm.

The sun was lower in the sky in this realm, since time ran differently here. The sunset spread in front of her. Streaks of gold crossed the sky with hints of pink and paler yellow, giving it depth. A weight lifted from her the farther she got from the desert, and she grinned contentedly. It was good to smile again.

Out of the corner of her eye, she noticed Piper staring at her, also beaming. "It's good to see you happy," said Piper.

"You aren't planning any romances for me, are you?"

"I don't plan romances. I only see if they could happen. Actually, well, I don't see any for you."

"Good," said Clara. "That's the best news I've had all day."

Piper's mouth fell open, but instead of asking for an explanation, she said, "I have a surprise for you." Then she walked away in a barefoot tiptoe walk that made the knee-length hem of her blue dress swing. Glancing back, she waved at Clara to follow.

Along the way, Clara noted all the changes to the ship. After the mess from a few months ago, and all the people needing temporary housing on Wave Sweeper, MacLir decided to do some upgrades. The bench MacLir was currently sitting on had previously made an L-shape around the mast. Now the benches were longer, and a third had been added, so three benches faced each other in a U-shape.

Heading into the cabin hallway, the sparkling green door on the left and the shimmery blue door on the right was the same, but now a third door in the middle glinted with hints of purple. Entering the new door led to a small room with only enough space for a bed and nightstand.

The whole room dripped purple in rich amethyst tones. From the purple and cream bedspread to amethysts embedded into the ceiling showing star constellations. A whole amethyst stone cut in half had been turned into a lamp base on the nightstand with a cream-colored shade. Based on the ship's green and blue rooms, identical in style, Clara assumed the door on the far wall led to the shared bathroom.

"We've added a mini room for you to come on adventures with us," said Piper.

With both hope and dread, she'd dreamed of a life without children to tend. A life without the type of responsibilities that stressed her out sounded blissful. Still, she was worried about being too alone. Her sister had offered to take her for a bit while she resettled, and now Piper was showing she'd be welcome here on their travels.

"Thank you, Piper, this is... so kind..." She wanted to say more, but emotion tightened her throat, and she fought to hold in tears. She rarely cried, especially in front of people.

Plastering on a smile, that for once she felt, she was about to try saying thank you better when Piper shouted, "Surprise!" Clara jumped at the noise. "I said surprise!" Piper said louder.

"I am very surprised—" Clara began, but Piper cut her off.

"No, no. Not you," she grumbled. Then, going to the bathroom door, she knocked loudly and shouted again, "Surprise!"

After the sound of a flush, the door swung wide, and Amy came out saying, "Keep your shirt on. You took too long, so I decided to actually use the bathroom."

"Amy!" Clara said, rushing over. She had no idea her baby sister was on board. This was a surprise. Clara was the oldest of eight girls and felt all of them were her children. Especially Amy, who she had practically raised alone as their mother became more forgetful.

They both strongly matched their mother in coloring with liquid chocolate eyes, dark brunette hair, and light brown skin. Their mother had been a great beauty in her day, as Amy was now with her full glossy lips and curvy frame. However, in features, Clara instead resembled her father's family in her thicker eyebrows and frizzy, wild, naturally curly hair.

When the three of them returned to the outdoor bench to enjoy the summer breeze and the sunset, MacLir excused himself to watch the baby and left the girls alone.

"Actually, I have something I want to talk about," began Piper.

"Always scheming," muttered Amy.

Clara tried not to laugh. Amy was not wholly wrong in that assessment. Piper had planned to get Amy pregnant and make her an immortal goddess of fertility simply to get her own child. It was a cold and calculated ploy that didn't consider Amy's feelings until further into the plan.

It had all worked out in the end, but now Piper was giving her a look that gave Clara a lot more sympathy for Amy's plight. Of course, Piper was the goddess of love, but Clara mused that she'd also make a good trickster god with how she meddled in people's lives.

"So, I represent the first stage of womanhood, The Maiden. Amy represents the second of the three, The Mother, although indirectly through her choice of Goddess of Creativity. However, there are three stages of womanhood."

"What is the third stage?" asked Clara.

"The Crone," she announced, glancing up and away, then hurried to add, "which is not as bad as it sounds. The Crone represents wisdom and endings. Endings are not always bad because they make way for the beginning I'm in charge of!"

Amy raised her hand like she was in a schoolroom. "So if the Maiden stands for beginnings and the Crone is endings, and I'm the Mother... what am I in charge of?"

"Maybe I should start again. The three aspects of womanhood are each special. I became the first in my ceremony, and Amy was the second. Each level has something to represent and power associated with it." Pausing for breath Piper continued, as if she'd memorized or rehearsed the words. "The Maiden is beginnings and love. The Mother is endurance and fertility. The Crone is endings and wisdom."

Amy snorted. "So, you are making new beginnings by helping them fall in love. And I make people pregnant, then help them endure?"

Clara laughed at Amy's tone. Her sister could always lighten her mood. "That is what mothers do. Endure one day at a time!" Clara said.

"No," said Piper, "you have it backward, Amy. You will give people the joy of a child, and the gift of family, which will help them endure life. Give them a reason to live."

Snorting, Clara shook her head. "Kids are great but don't help a stressful living situation. Besides, women have way more things to live for."

Piper sighed, then hesitated, searching for words. "Well, it's what Brigit told me. Maybe I got the words wrong. But, other than the screaming and diapers, I'm enjoying my time with Emily. Adding a third member will make our goddess-hood complete and stronger."

With a sinking feeling that she might be able to guess why this topic came up, Clara asked, "So, where are you going to find a crone to complete your trio?"

"Well, I was thinking of you," said Piper.

Clara sighed internally. She wanted a quiet life for a while, without responsibilities or entanglements. She didn't know what they wanted her to do but knew it would be something, and anything was already too much. "If Brigit is keen, why can't she be the crone?"

"She's not old enough," said Piper, tucking her feet under her dress as the sun finished disappearing and the night became cooler.

"Isn't she three thousand years old?"

"Well, no. It's more like three hundred because of the time difference, and she's already a goddess of healing and fertility, so she can't be our crone. Besides, she doesn't look old," pointed out Piper.

"Are you saying I look old?" Clara asked. She knew no good way to answer the question as soon as it was out of her mouth.

She felt terrible for putting Piper in a situation where she'd have to struggle for a reply. She immediately took back her worry when Piper simply replied, "Yes."

Clara wanted to feel insulted but was honest enough to acknowledge that she felt old sometimes, even though she was only in her mid-forties. White strands sprinkled her hair, early laugh lines wrinkled her face, and the thickening around her middle was permanent. She was no longer a spring chicken.

She also understood Piper's autism might mean she didn't notice that now would have been a time to tell a white lie gracefully. In fact, Clara didn't always catch those moments unless she was prepared for them by someone else. A crone, though? Ouch.

Amy had been suspiciously quiet during the bombardment of information. Like she'd already heard the speech and was letting it play out. "So, I assume you want this too?" Clara asked her.

Shrugging, Amy said, "It would give you some purpose, and it would make us all stronger in our visions. It might be fun to have a little club, just the three of us. Mostly it would mean you could stay with me longer. Either way, it's time for bed, so we can finish our chat in the morning after you've slept on the idea."

Amy covered her mouth with a big yawn, and Piper pressed one last time, "What do you think about being part of the three?"

"I'll think about it," Clara said and meant it. However, she was still unsure if she wanted to get tangled in magic, especially immortality like Amy had accepted. Old injuries in her ankle and knee had caused both to stiffen as she sat in the cold night air, and as the three friends made their way to the cabin door, she shuffled along the wooden deck. "If I decide to officially become a crone, at least I've got the walk down."

CHAPTER 2

Piper

Water dripped down the rough cave walls creating a muddy spot across the floor of the underground tunnel. The dim, invisible lights on the low ceiling created a soft, diffuse glow that helped Piper see where to put her feet. The tunnel connected the many faerie mounds with higher ceilings, like the feasting hall or the kitchens. She'd learned the faerie mounds in Ireland were grass-covered hills that dotted the island. Some were built as fortifications by kings of the land, and others were made for a king's burial. They were all created so long ago that legends formed around them over the years. It was said if they were desecrated, the fairies would enforce a curse on the trespasser.

Scared of making the fairies angry, the mounds were left alone through the centuries and had become part of the human realm landscape. A landscape mirrored in the faerie realm that MacLir's creation legends made him the guardian over. She often visited the mounds and connected tunnels when she first discovered the faeries and gods, but never something she enjoyed.

While Piper generally preferred low light, she didn't like the closeness of the walls down here. Worse, politics among the fae group known as the Tuatha Dé Danann had created chaos not too long ago. Lies spread about MacLir had made the tunnels briefly dangerous for the two of them.

The uprising was quelled, and MacLir had been more visible around the mound tunnels to reassure people and bolster the new High Court. Unfortunately, that meant bringing Piper and the new baby because with time so sped up in the Otherworld, he might accidentally come home to a toddler if he lost track of time here.

The infant in her arms felt heavy. She considered passing it off to MacLir, but Emily was blessedly quiet for the moment, and Piper didn't want to wake her. Besides, three more turns and they'd be in the kitchens. After a quick word with the head cook, they'd pop out the kitchen entrance where they left Wave Sweeper.

Piper squinted as something caught her eye. They were approaching a bend in the corridor, and it looked like someone peeked around the edge and ducked back. Piper's heart raced. MacLir had been attacked several times when everything was at its worst. Brigit had warned them that things here were still simmering. People were upset.

Glancing over at MacLir, she met his gaze, and he nodded. He'd seen it too. Shifting the baby slightly, Piper felt around in the crossbody diaper bag she wore these days. The flashlight she finally found reassured her. She kept a tight hold on it in case the mysterious figure turned the corner.

A group waited for them. Quickly counting heads, Piper thought it was about ten men and women. All were in mud-streaked, ragged clothes except for a clean new armband of solid brown cloth. "For Ian!" they shouted as the destitute Tua De rushed forward, many waving kitchen knives.

MacLir put himself in front of Piper, giving the group time to cut off their retreat and herd them into the corner. Then, not wanting to leave Piper and Emily alone, he let them approach.

The boldest with a knife stepped forward. "If I kill you, I get to live where I want. I can move above ground again," the man said.

"Actually, I'm not in charge of that," said MacLir, his boyish voice gentle and soothing, adding, "It's your own laws you should be trying to change."

"Lies," hissed a woman from the crowd. "Ian told us the truth."

A man beside her said, "Because of you, MacLir, we can't live under the sun anymore."

"MacLir has held us in the dark for too long," agreed someone in the back.

Piper had previously heard the last two phrases shouted by protesters. It had been months ago in human realm time, but technically only a week or so had passed here, and tensions they had hoped to calm were still running high.

Spreading his hands out, palm up, MacLir said, "Please let us pass. Hurting us won't help your situation. You are all young enough to have been born here in the caves, so perhaps you don't know your full history. Go talk to the new High Court about your requests."

"No more talking," said the first man. With those words, the group surged forward again.

Piper wished MacLir had considered this might happen and brought his swords. Then no one would have bothered them. Instead, she watched him punch the attackers lower, making them double over in pain, putting them in range of a knockout punch.

All her attention was on the man that got past MacLir and was heading straight for her. She launched forward with one arm outstretched, the other arm keeping her baby as far away as possible, and jabbed the hidden taster end of the flashlight into his neck. Pushing a button gave the fae a high-voltage electric shock.

As they'd practiced while the attacker was distracted, Piper said, "MacLir, got one!" The stunned man was shaking off the effects when MacLir swept his feet out from under him, then kicked him in the head. He lay still, and MacLir returned to the final knife wielders not on the ground yet.

Piper braced for the next guy, pleased with how well her new tool worked and what a great team they made. Another quickly slipped through, a slim sallow man stalking forward with no weapon except an intense stare.

Brandishing her flashlight, she was shocked when it sailed from her hand and fell a foot away. She looked up to see a man with his arm outstretched. The flashlight continued to inch away from Piper, leaving her to face him alone. Except she wasn't alone. In their practices, anytime she couldn't handle it on her own, she was supposed to call for MacLir. If she wasn't calling out, he could focus on the fight in front of him.

Trying to call for help, she was alarmed when no sound came out. Her throat simply didn't work. In fact, nothing worked. She was locked in place. Piper never considered the blood running through her until it felt like it slowed. She wondered if this was one of the blood magic Tua De she'd heard about. Or was something else keeping her from moving at all?

Her brain went fuzzy, and her vision blurred. She saw MacLir pick up her small weapon through the haze and race over. Fury blazed in his usually calm aqua eyes. He zapped the man repeatedly until he doubled over. The hold over Piper vanished, and in the loosening of her muscles, she gripped Emily tighter, worried that she might drop her. Instead, the shift woke the infant, who howled about the injustice of an interrupted nap.

MacLir returned his attention to his fight and got a face full of coins. The metal hit his forehead and nose, clattered to the ground, and vanished. One man held out his palm where the handful of old large coins reappeared, but he didn't throw them again. The last three standing were hanging back. Far enough to show hesitation but close enough to still be a threat.

"You can leave," said MacLir, breathing heavily. "I won't follow you, and you will escape punishment. Just leave now."

"We are making life better for our clans," said the woman to the two men.

They repeated the mantra together as all three charged forward. MacLir sighed and raised his fists, bloody and bruised. Blood was also splattered into his blond hair and dripped from cuts on his arms and back. He didn't seem to notice. As they got close, MacLir dodged the coins, which put him directly in the path of the woman suddenly holding a thick tree branch with dark summer leaves still attached.

She began beating MacLir with it, the leaves detaching and floating in the air around them. He ignored the hits to get in close and stun her arm with the electric shock flashlight. She cried out, the spasming muscles in her arm causing her to drop the branch.

Distracted by the leaf lady and the coin guy, MacLir didn't notice the last man pick up one of the knives off the ground and edge toward Piper. Still sluggish from the previous hold over her, she tried to run but found her legs were too shaky. She tried to call out, but only a squeak emerged from her tight throat. Then, turning away from the man to shield her screaming baby, she braced for the impact of a kitchen knife in her back.

Out of the corner of her eye, she saw a flash of long flowing fur. Watching the dog's leap, she saw how close the knife man had come. The dog's teeth landed firmly in the man's arm. He screamed and tripped, dropping the knife as he landed hard on the damp dirt floor. The tall hunting dog gave him a shake, then released him to take a defensive stance in front of Piper.

The knife man backed up and ran. Cradling his injured arm, he touched the coin guy's arm as he went, and the two of them sped down the tunnel and out of sight around a corner, leaving anyone who fell to lay in the mud.

Finally finding her voice, Piper reached out a hand to let the dog sniff her and said, "Thank you."

A bubbling feeling in her brain let her know the animal was speaking, then the words dripped in, bit by bit. "I heard the baby crying and got here as soon as I could. I was trained as a protector for my master's children."

"Your master must appreciate your help," replied Piper in the same way as the dog, mind-to-mind.

"That was many years ago in England. Those kids are grown and gone. I have no master now."

Unaware she was talking to the large dog, MacLir said, "Piper, can you move yet? We need to leave." Still, on high alert, he was watching both hallways, his shoulders tense.

Talking to animals was another power she was finally growing used to, and it had come in handy to speak with her kitten Flutter. Piper transferred the finally quiet baby to her other arm and sent the thought, "Where do you live?"

"Here and there. You smell of Brigit. She gives me food sometimes."

Quickly deciding there was room on the ship for both her cat and a dog, she sent, "Would you like to come live with us? A warm home with a new child to protect."

The dog agreed, and Piper filled MacLir in on the rough details of the dog as he led them through the last few tunnels. The dog trotted beside Piper and Emily, as wary and alert as MacLir.

Eventually reaching the kitchen, MacLir waved off assistance with a tight smile and hustled Piper through the kitchen archways. Grabbing her free hand and resting his larger hand on the dog's back, he walked them through the wall. Piper saw a flash of dirt, then roots, and finally grass. The fastest transition she'd ever witnessed.

Not letting go of her, MacLir nearly dragged them to Wave Sweeper. After taking Emily, he pushed Piper toward the rope ladder and followed with the infant. At the top, he looked down and said, "I assume you want the dog?"

"Yes, please," said Piper, "I'm going to keep her."

"Another female on my ship," fake grumbled MacLir with a laugh, passing the child off as he headed back down the ladder. Moments later, he reappeared at the top again, carrying a large dog with gorgeous red fur.

Piper had not been able to see the dog well in the dark tunnels, but now she handed Emily back to MacLir to put in bed and sat cross-legged on the deck next to the dog who rescued them.

Her slightly curving tail wagged gently. Intelligent chocolate brown eyes examined Piper from a long face tipped with a black nose. Blood from the attack crusted around her mouth, but it was hard to see with her coloring already red. The beautiful auburn fur was muddy and matted in places, but enough shown through that Piper was sure her guess of a red setter breed was correct. White patches around her eyes and ears showed her age but didn't make her any less regal.

"You are beautiful," she thought to the dog.

"Not as pretty as I once was," sighed the dog, grave and matter-of-fact.

Piper thanked the setter again as exhaustion finally caught up with her. All she wanted was rest, still shaky from the loss of adrenaline after almost dying twice today. Deciding she could not leave her rescuer in such an uncomfortable state. So she led their new family member to the bathroom to clean up.

Hazel

Slipping the dress over her head Hazel admired herself in the mirror. The baby blue tones of the airy plus-sized dress matched nicely with her peach skin. She frowned at the puffy capped sleeves. She'd liked them in the past, but they seemed childish to her now.

The price tag knotted her wispy hair as she pulled the dress off again. She growled at it. Her hair was always tangling into things, even itself.

"What are you snarling about over there?" asked her best friend from one changing room stall over. "How is the blue dress?"

"Not my thing," replied Hazel.

"How 'bout this one?"

Hazel laughed as a bit of cloth flew over the wall, which turned into a squeal as she held it up. "Red! My favorite!"

Her mother had told Hazel red clashed with her strawberry blond hair, but what did she know? Living in the fairy mounds all her life, how could her mother give fashion advice?

The red summer dress made her feel pretty, she decided after putting it on. Somehow, it made her feel like a real teenager, like one from the human realm. Besides, it sucked in some of her chubby curves, and she decided it looked great with her hair. Definitely a dress she'd be taking home.

Bursting out of the stall, she bumped into her friend, and they both squealed in delight at how amazing they looked. So different from anything else worn in the clan. Her family was a group that had not visited the human world since top hats were in style.

The last member of their trio came out of the stall behind Hazel. She was also in a summer dress, but one with a flared skirt and puffed sleeves. Hazel felt superior that her red knee-length dress had the thin straps over the shoulders often seen in the style magazines.

"How long have we been here?" their third wheel asked nervously.

"Honestly, Tarla. Who cares if we're late getting back?" Hazel asked the question with all the boldness she could gather and was pleased with the result. However, a hint of worry she kept pushing away still reminded her that they needed to return before dinner.

"It's just... it feels like more than ten minutes," the slightly younger girl muttered.

That was another thing that annoyed her. The time difference between realms meant that after all the trouble it took to get here, they could only spend ten minutes shopping and five minutes getting a snack. She loved the shopping centers that Americans called malls. If she was allowed to do what she wanted, she'd move to America and practically live in a shopping mall.

America was a distant dream, though. All she wanted was to live like a human. They had everything she didn't, from the malls and snacks, to sunshine and money. Tarla, as half-human, was allowed to live here one day. There was no hope for Hazel.

"Are these the dresses we want?" her best friend asked, ever in charge.

"Yes, Emma," said Tarla meekly, and they returned to the stalls to change out of their new clothes.

"It's my turn," said Emma, leading them out of the fitting room and marching directly to the check-out clerk. Her brown curls bounced, and her hips swayed suggestively in a dress from a different shopping day. The boy their age watched her approach, mesmerized first by her appearance, then by her green eyes. "You like me," she told the boy.

He nodded enthusiastically.

"I like this dress," she said. "I'm going to take it with me, and I've already paid for it."

He nodded but less emphatically.

"I'm going now. You will not remember my friends or me as soon as we are out of your sight."

The boy's nod was barely perceptible. His eyes were completely glazed over.

Emma left the boy staring into space, drool dripping down one corner of his open mouth. She waved her compatriots onward, and the green glow drained from her eyes once they were at the door. Released from the spell, the boy coughed and looked around, but by then, Hazel and her friends were outside the storefront, stolen dresses in hand, and the clerk didn't recognize them.

With a twinge of guilt, Hazel wondered if this was why the High Court had rules about her people not living with humans. They were so easily manipulated. Of course, if the Tua De were simply allowed to live here with real jobs, she wouldn't have to run off with dresses. Besides, the High Court didn't care a fig about humans, so there must be some other reason she had to live in an underground hovel.

Making their way to the outskirts of town and into a forest the locals thought was haunted, the girls found the tall hedge. They prepared to go home by bundling their modern clothes with the new dresses.

Changing back into her high-waisted and full-length printed cotton dress, Hazel sighed at the necessity of it. She wanted to wear her new clothes, but knew that would draw attention. Like much of her permitted wardrobe, this dress was one her rake-thin mother had worn as a youth. Although the seams had been adjusted to fit Hazel, they still felt too tight and constricting. Especially after trying on all the flowy floral summer dresses, she loved so much.

Finding the shimmery spot between two trees, she hesitated before following her friends through it. The thought of stepping forward took away the air in her lungs. The closeness of the ceiling, the lack of light, the rules… it was all suffocating her slowly.

Not for the first time, she considered running away. She was in the human world right now. She could simply stay, said one part of her mind. The other part reminded her of Tarla's detailed explanations about birth certificates, passports, and taxes. Most of it had not made much sense. Humans seemed to complicate everything.

She knew as the minutes of her indecision ticked by here her friends were waiting much longer on their end. If they had not already given up waiting. She'd stalled here before. All she was doing was making herself late, and just like the other times, she finally gave in and stepped forward.

The forest faded as she began traveling back by sliding down a dirt and rock tunnel. Finally, it dumped her out in a small cave. Standing, she sighed and brushed off as much dirt as she could.

Stalking home through muddy tunnels, she came across a handful of men and women on the ground. They looked asleep, but were sprawled at odd angles. From the state of their shabby clothes, she knew they were outcasts. The clanless and jobless that survived on the one free meal a day provided by MacLir through the fairy kitchens and slept in the hallways by night.

It was impossible to tell the time here, but she knew it couldn't be night yet. She had not lingered in the human world that long. Stepping over the sleeping forms blocking the curve in the tunnel, she decided they must have gone to the human realm for a little of what her father called the black stuff. For a clan priding itself on never breaking the rules, her father and his buddies had beer often enough. They also passed out drunk regularly.

Arriving in the large round common room of their clan, no one commented on her tardiness. Relieved that she was probably on time, she veered left and entered one of the small carved-out spaces where her family lived. The area was filled with a front room, a bedroom, and a tiny cooking alcove.

At some point, the small suite was obviously made for one person, but now it housed her parents in the bedroom, and she shared the front room with her grandmama.

"Hazel! You missed dinner. Where have you been?" Demanded her mother as soon as the curtain fell behind her. Surely the people out in the common room could hear them, but in a space so cramped, everyone politely pretended they couldn't.

She must have stood lost in thought in the forest for longer than she realized. Oh, well. She was tired of this. Shaking her clothing bundle at her mother, she said, "Who cares? I'm not hungry and too young to join the real feast anyway."

The red dress picked that moment to slip free from the bundle and slink to the ground. Hazel's mother darted forward and picked it up. "What are you bringing home, now?"

"Another dress from Tarla. She didn't want it anymore."

"That girl gets rid of a lot of clothes," said her mother while holding up the dress. "There's almost nothing to this! No sleeves and one stiff breeze will show off your underpants!"

"We don't have any wind down here," said Hazel.

Her mother ignored the comment, holding out a price tag on the dress. "A dress she didn't want anymore?" asked her mother knowingly with a raised eyebrow. "Besides, that little half-magic mouse of a girl would never wear something so bright or revealing. You didn't get all the dirt off your skirt, and I know those streaks. You went to the human world, didn't you?"

Hazel was half scared of her mother's upcoming retaliation and half angry at continually being treated like a child. So what if she'd gone to the other realm? No one would tell her why that was bad, and she was sick of her mother's arbitrary rules.

In the silence, her mother started the familiar rant. How humans were stupid and dangerous. How Hazel's family was lucky to have a small safe space inside a larger clan community passed down to them. It was too much this time, and Hazel's tolerance snapped.

"Safe? Oh sure, safe underground, but away from the sun and the wider world." The thought brought back the unfairness and the boiling rage she felt about it. Why could no one explain why they were hiding down here? She often asked, but never got an answer. So she tried again. "Safe from what?"

"You're just bored," said her mom, predictably changing the subject.

"I'm not bored. I'm mad."

"Bored," her mother intoned pointedly, an attempt to end the discussion. "Take up a job in the kitchens like your father and me. You'll see we have a good life here. I was like you once, I visited the human world, but it's perilous for us there."

Hazel had never before wondered where the old-fashioned dresses had come from. Clearly, her mother had spent time with the humans yet dared deny her daughter the same chance to see some of the wonders she must have enjoyed?

She considered the growing collection of dresses stashed under her bed. What if one day Hazel would have to pathetically try to make them fit her own daughter? The mental image put her in a worse mood and brought back the tightness in her chest. The ceiling crowded in, feeling lower than ever.

"I might go back to the human world with Emma and just stay there," Hazel threatened, but knew she'd made a mistake as soon as the words were out of her mouth. She'd both admitted to breaking the rules by visiting the other realm and, somewhat worse in her mother's eyes, revealed her continued friendship with the daughter of a rival clan.

"Emma," said her mother, her tone quiet and seething. "I've told you over and over not to spend time with that girl. She's nothing but trouble, and I'll not have you seen with her. Do you understand?"

Pressing her lips tightly together, she glared at her mother in silent challenge.

"That's it. You are not allowed to leave the cave for a week. I'll bring your meals here. If you argue now, your punishment will only be worse."

Glancing around, Hazel took in her bedridden grandmama, also giving her disapproving looks and her father staring into his beer mug. Finally, her gaze fell on her bed out in the open, where she'd have to sit for a week. The lack of private space was maddening at the best of times, but she couldn't survive a week within these tight rock walls.

Worse, never seeing Emma again. A memory floated to the top of her mind of an invite from Emma that she'd turned down. It was for tonight to attend a youth gathering in one of the meeting halls. It was after her curfew, so she turned it down, but now?

There was no way she could follow these new rules her mother had laid on her, so if she wasn't going to follow those two, what was the point in following any of the rules? She turned on one slippered foot and walked away, leaving her mother holding the red dress in the middle of their cave.

"Come back here and finish talking to me! Where do you think you are going?"

Too mad to answer, Hazel stomped out of the common room, back down the tunnels, and all the way to the fairy mound's meeting spaces.

CHAPTER 3

Hazel

She heard the music first. Upbeat and modern. Nothing like the stringed instruments played during the feasts. The closer she got, the clearer it became until it was almost uncomfortably loud. However, now that she was in the meeting room, the music was nearly drowned out by the voices of more Tua De youth than she'd ever seen in one place. At least a thousand.

Teens from all the clans chatted in groups, painted protest signs, or danced to the music. She didn't see a single adult.

Overwhelmed with where to go after making it through the doorway, she was grateful to see Emma running over to her. She looked fantastic in the new orange dress she'd picked out and gleamed with happiness. "You came! You said you couldn't make it," said Emma, giving Hazel a hug.

"I couldn't miss this," said Hazel overly loud, wondering if she could be heard over the din. She felt frumpy in her out-of-date cotton and wished she'd grabbed one of her new dresses. Or, better yet, ripped the new dress out of her mother's grasp on the way out.

"Come on," said Emma, taking Hazel's hand and dragging her into the thick of things. Her hand was warm, and even though Hazel knew warmth was not Emma's power, it felt like the heat of their clasped hands radiated through her. This was one of the nicer meeting rooms, with wall-to-wall wood floors and a stage for performances. No mud here.

Emma kneeled in front of a board. She continued decorating around the words, "We're fighting for our future." Waving for Hazel to join her, Emma placed a blank white sign in front of her, and someone else tossed her a thick marker. It clattered on the wooden boards under them.

She wanted to ask what this party was about, but it was so loud, and everyone seemed to already know. Also, she didn't want to look ignorant in front of Emma. So she doodled on the corners while straining to hear the conversation and glean what might be best to write and what these signs were for.

She was finally about to break down and ask when the music stopped. A young woman walked on stage. Her boots thumping with every step silenced the crowd. Almost an adult, but not entirely, she was classic Tua De in her coloring of pale skin, dark brown hair, and vibrant green eyes. Wearing tight jeans and a cropped, long-sleeved tee shirt, she was comfortable in modern human clothes. A blue armband stood out against her yellow shirt.

A spotlight shone down on her where she stood alone at center stage. She raised a microphone and, in a calm, measured tone, said, "We are here to work together. It's the only way we can make progress. First, we must show we're willing to act."

The crowd exploded with clapping, and when it quieted, she continued, "We want change. We want what Ian promised us. Instead, they murdered him and replaced his government. The High Court won't even speak with us because they say we're too young to understand. Well, I say, they're too old to understand!"

The crowd's cheer was deafening, with lots of whistling and shouting above the clapping. Hazel agreed wholeheartedly. This is what she'd been saying for ages. If her antique parents could only comprehend. The human world may have been bad in the past, but that has changed.

"We can move past petty clan disagreements. We're above the clans. We are the Tua De of the future! We're all one people who have the power to make changes. We can work together and solve the issues. We're going to get our golden era back!"

She spread her arms wide with a huge smile, and the crowd's roar was twice as loud as before. Hazel barely heard it. Her thoughts raced with these new ideas. Could the other young people like her make their own clan? Could they actually change the High Court's mind? Or, better change out the whole High Court. She imagined the woman on stage in the role of High King. Women were not allowed, but maybe that could be changed. Hazel would vote this woman in as High Queen in a heartbeat. She clapped and shouted with everyone else as the woman bowed and stepped aside.

A boy took the stage next, accepting the mic from the girl. His stance was more hesitant. He waited for the crowd to calm as the first speaker finally made her way off the stage. "In our golden era, we were craftsmen, musicians, farmers, and warriors. A race of kings. Each of us was worth the admiration of the humans who served us."

He paused, and a murmur went through the crowd as if everyone agreed by commenting to the people surrounding them. Emma leaned in close to Hazel and whispered, "I like Ariana's speeches best, but this guy always makes some good points."

Hazel nodded, trying not to show how the sound waves of Emma's voice had tickled her ear. Or how the warmth of

Emma's breath on her neck had sent heat racing through her again. The heady feeling of being so near Emma while new knowledge poured through her brain was dizzying.

The young man stepped forward and sat on the edge of the stage. His dangling legs almost distracted Hazel from his following words. "Extreme poverty happens when a group of people has nothing to trade and no income. We had everything, and it was taken from our great-grandparents by humans. So now we are dealing with a new generation growing up in distress. Us. And it's not fair."

Hazel thought of her bed so close to her grandmama's snoring. The ever-present mud. They were grateful for the scraps of food for breakfast and lunch, knowing that others had nothing to eat except dinner.

"Humans robbed us of our home. They stole our culture, becoming craftsmen, musicians, farmers, and warriors in our place. Peace with humans is impossible. They must finally pay for their treachery. Then we can live in the sun again."

Hazel remembered the shiny shopping center. Light filtering in through glass ceilings. Humans lived like that all the time. Hazel didn't have The Sight, but her mind created a hopeful glimpse of a possible future in which she lived in a sunlit house with wood floors like the one she was standing on. No parents, no rules, no mud.

The boy on the stage stood and shouted, "The time for the young to take control is now. It's time to march. Tonight we make our voices heard!" He raised the microphone, punching the air above him, his other fist thrust high to join it.

The crowd cheered for a long moment, then began to prepare. Everyone swarmed over the large room, cleaning up tables and snacks, packing up the speakers from the music, and putting the finishing touches on signs.

Hazel knelt next to her blank sign. This time, she knew what to write. She wrote in letters as big as she could make them, "No one can keep me from living under the sun."

Piper

"It was impossible to get anywhere for two hours. Over a thousand rioting youth jammed all the connecting tunnels and waved signs at anyone trying to get through," said Brigit. Her perfect dark curls and silvery goddess dress seemed out of place in Amy's cozy kitchen. She pinched a piece of toast awkwardly between two fingers to butter it.

As if she'd never prepared food before, thought Piper. Food prep was something she was finally getting the hang of, so she considered offering Brigit a hand, but the spectacle was too funny to watch. Even if the topic of conversation was serious.

"What did the kids want?" Clara asked, while expertly draining a whole pot of pasta with only the pot lid.

"It was all the same cult stuff Ian's followers were saying, but now the youth somehow have ahold of it. The ideals are too pervasive. Like before, I mostly agree with some of it," sighed Brigit, dropping the toast on the pan and starting to butter another. Then rushed to add, "Not all of it, of course."

Piper assumed all four women were thinking about Brigit's past betrayal in the careful silence after her comment. Lucky had told everyone he forgave Brigit for handing him over to their enemies because she didn't know what would happen. MacLir forgave her for directing them to an ambush using the same reasoning. However, Piper was not totally willing to forgive so easily.

Since no one else seemed ready to talk about it, she kept her mouth shut in case she said something wrong. Piper examined her fingernails but looked up through her eyelashes to watch the others. Clara twirled a pot lid. Amy focused on the vegetables she was slicing. Brigit placed the last pieces of toast on the tray.

Finally, Brigit said, "So, I'm considering moving out of the tunnels and into the human realm. I wouldn't technically be breaking the law if I lived with Lucky since he's a half-magic and allowed to live here."

Relieved to have a safer topic, Piper asked, "Where are you thinking of living?"

"We're not sure. Maybe here in Dublin? Or, in one of the coastal towns near the main fairy mound."

"I need a place to live, too," stated Clara. She'd pulled bowls down to dish out the plain pasta, with a spoonful of sauce on each.

Amy came behind, adding vegetables to each meal and saying, "You can stay here as long as you want. It's nice having you around."

"This apartment is on the small side," said Clara, putting a hand on her sister's shoulder. "Especially with two dogs underfoot. It feels like I'm constantly stepping on one of them."

"Same!" laughed Amy. Then, turning to Piper, she said, "I can't imagine how you'll manage on Wave Sweeper when Emily starts crawling. Its cabin is smaller than our little home, even with MacLir's magic to make it bigger on the inside."

Piper hadn't considered when Emily would move around. What if she climbed the edge of the ship? Especially where it dipped lower at the top of the rope ladder. She wondered if she needed to move too. Maybe MacLir could find them a rental to raise Emily in, at least until she was old enough not to tip overboard.

Piper realized she would enjoy living near Clara or Amy and wondered if she should also choose Dublin. Since they wanted to move too, she wouldn't mind living with them if the house was big enough to hold them comfortably. An idea bubbled into Piper's brain. Elusive, but there. She just had to catch it.

MacLir interrupted her thoughts when he grabbed her from behind in a big hug. A wave of clean salty air washed over her. She smiled to herself and leaned back against him.

Robin greeted Amy similarly, with less vigor and a brief hello kiss.

Lucky made his way over to Brigit and bumped her shoulder. She smiled over at him.

As a goddess of love, Piper was keenly aware that Clara was without a mate. She cut her eyes over to the older woman as nonchalantly as she could, but the smile on Clara's face seemed natural.

Deciding again to give up romance for Clara, at least for a while, she let MacLir pull her off the bar stool and into a real hug. The couple of visions she'd tried since Clara arrived in Ireland still showed her alone and seemingly happy about it.

Emily, on the other hand, she was already getting visions about. She could not help peeking. Her daughter would blossom into an imaginative and fearless young woman. So very much a sea god's daughter. While it was nothing Piper could influence yet, if everything stayed lined up, Emily would likely fall in love with Brigit and Lucky's son one day.

While she daydreamed, Clara and Amy had efficiently loaded the dining table with food and called her over. After one last glance at Emily, she wandered to a spot next to MacLir at the table. She considered how, with this group of people, she felt comfortable allowing herself to become lost in thought or be late to the table.

With anyone else, she'd be stressed out. On high alert to make sure she was doing everything correctly. Saying the right things or acting the right way. Not here, though. This table full of mixed-up found family had accepted her as she accepted them. "These dinner parties are not often enough," she said aloud, almost to herself.

"Agreed," said Amy. "We'll do them more if everyone settles nearby."

The comment tickled the idea in Piper's brain, the one she was trying to have before. The thought of everyone eating at each other's houses, the image of the babies growing up near each other, and how everyone was looking for a new place to live. Then it snapped together. The solution.

"Aha!" Piper said. "I've got it."

"Got what?" MacLir asked, a smile just for her crinkling the corners of his sea-blue eyes.

The vision in her mind was so perfect that it was hard to describe. Where to begin? No one asked again or rushed her into speaking. They knew she'd talk when she was ready. She took a bite of her food and then another. Organizing her words, she took a deep breath and said, "Let's live together. All seven of us, with our kids and pets. Here's what I'm thinking."

They ate food and sipped wine while she outlined her vision. Four houses were built around a square block of land. Custom for each family, and would have interior doors on each end of the houses to connect to the other homes. In Piper's imagination, the four houses were so spacious that they met at the corners, forming a courtyard in the center large enough to hold a parking spot for Wave Sweeper, a garden, and a playground.

After clearing plates out of the way, Amy handed out paper to everyone, and they spent the next few hours wrapped up in drawing and comparing sketches of plans. At one point, Clara asked, "How will we pay for this? Some of the best things in life are free, but houses are not one of them." She chuckled to herself, a smile touching her lips.

Piper waived her question away, saying, "That's something we never have to worry about."

"One of my hobbies is lost treasure," clarified MacLir. "I can hear the prayers sent to the god of the sea by any name they call me, but I can't save them all, and some don't bother with prayer. Old ships provide treasure and antiques, while newer ones have things like wine and jewelry. I sell bits of it as I need to. With Piper's idea of a four-house mansion, we'll have to sell a lot of it."

CHAPTER 4

Clara

"After her bath, she had a pleasantly doggy scent. Also, it revealed silky fur and long soft ears," called down Piper.

Clara eased up the rope ladder, noting how effortlessly Piper clambered above her. She remembered having that much energy. A long time ago.

At the top, Clara was enthusiastically greeted by a gorgeous elderly red dog. A new wide dark green collar held a shiny name tag. "Vixen," said Clara, "cute name."

"She told me that's what her first master called her, and she's used to the name. She's promised to guard Emily. So, with Vixen's permission, we've been feeding her little bits of Pig, so she'll be around as Emily grows up."

"That's a lovely idea," said Clara, wishing she had a companion as brave and loyal as Emily would have.

MacLir came up the ladder next, slower than usual, while holding his daughter. The dog's curved tail wagged happily as everyone sat on the bench, then she settled at their feet.

"So, did you want to talk about anything specific, or you just needed time away from Amy's house?" Piper asked.

"Both, actually," replied Clara. "Robin might appreciate having Amy to himself for a while, and I have some questions about your offer. I was all for pushing Amy to become an Irish goddess when you wanted her to do it. Now though, it's me you are pushing. I have questions."

MacLir answered what he could about magic, what powers would be like for Clara, and what powers people ended up with and why. However, he had trouble answering her questions about how powers work in connection to Ireland. Also, how magic exists, where it comes from, and why both humans and Tua De have it, along with other magical beings like elementals.

"I surrender," said MacLir with a laugh as he stood to go to bed. "I guess we don't know as much as we thought." He and Piper waved goodnight as they headed into the cabin.

Clara stayed seated long after they left, soaking in all the information she'd received. It was likely she would go ahead with the ceremony. She'd let Piper know in the morning, but becoming immortal was separate. Standing, she stretched her stiff joints by wandering to the ship's edge to look out over the water.

Surprised to see a massive creature in the water below her, she jumped. It startled, too, trying to both flee and see who was standing on the deck. Then, finally, it shifted higher, saying, "Hello, crone."

Not a crone yet, Clara wanted to reply. She had heard of the dragon Fia from Piper. A clairvoyant who could sometimes see the future, this scaled water creature with snake fangs could not be anyone else. Yet looked suspiciously like an eavesdropper. "You seem up to something."

Their blue and green iridescent scales rippled, and the fading late-night summer light caught hints of purple. "I would never hurt Piper," replied the sea dragon.

"Oddly specific," said Clara. "Who would you hurt?"

The dragon's tail lashed like an irritated cat, then they sunk into the water without a splash. Only a spreading ripple on the surface showed Clara that she had not imagined it.

Hazel

A foam mattress cradled her body, and a feather pillow did the same for her head. Hazel opened her eyes and enjoyed all over again the visual luxury that was Emma's room.

Plush rugs were laid over soft cream carpets with heavy gold and cream matching furniture. Cream-colored wallpaper lined the space, leaving room for a nearly sheer curtain-covered window. A glow came from behind the curtains, and Hazel could almost imagine it was sunlight instead of a flat heat lamp.

Emma was there beside her, a warm presence during the last couple of nights. When Hazel didn't want to go home after the rally, Emma invited her to a sleepover.

Hazel had never been to Emma's home before and was shocked to find it was an actual house built inside a cave. Emma said many homes like it were built for high-ranking officials or clan heads. Hazel had been in her clean leader's home, and it was barely larger than the tiny hole her family lived in. She had no idea these kinds of spaces existed underground.

If she'd seen this place before the rally, she would have been a tiny bit jealous. Now though, she knew one day soon they'd get the rules changed, and she could live in a real house in the human realm. With her mind opened to how much was wrong with the mounds, she was excited about the plans to change the situation.

Hazel had offered to sleep on the floor in Emma's room, because even the carpet looked more comfortable than her own thin spring-filled mattress on a stone slab.

Instead, Emma welcomed Hazel to her bed, and her

mind was opened to even more possibilities than she'd imagined before the rally. Both new experiences were tied in her mind, a whole night of excitement and firsts. When Emma said another event was happening and shyly asked if Hazel wanted to go, the answer was an enthusiastic yes.

Hazel didn't realize she'd been staring at Emma sleeping until the other girl woke. Emma's giddy smile was mirrored on her own face, and they shared a good morning kiss before getting ready for today's event.

Meeting during the day, the gathering was much calmer than the evening rally. No loud music or drinks. No one shouting into microphones. An unfamiliar boy wearing a blue armband was sitting at a table and checking people in at the door. As several more people arrived, he announced, "This meeting is for the initiated or those here to sign up for initiation."

Emma grabbed her hand and tugged her into the line to check-in. "Are you initiated?" Hazel asked.

"No, but it sounds like fun. Let's do it together," said Emma. It was half command but said with such a big smile that Hazel could not say no. Besides, she planned to support the group's ideals, so she might as well officially join them.

The line moved slowly, but Emma had not let go of her hand, and they chatted easily while they waited. Hazel was still amazed by the recent turn of events. They'd been friends for years, and the new closeness had only deepened their friendship.

After they gave the man their names, he asked them a list of questions. Most were easily answered. Both girls replied no when the final question was asked, "Do you have any human blood in your family line?" However, a sliver of concern objected in the back of Hazel's mind. She had said no, though if they checked, she wondered what they'd find.

She'd once heard her grandmama talking about an ancestor who was the daughter of a firbolg tribe. She'd never been brave enough to ask if that was a human tribe or another name for a distant Tua De clan. The way her mother shushed her grandmama made Hazel think they were probably not proud of it. Also, it would explain the tint of red to her hair, which was unusual in her community.

Also, after seeing how Emma's family lived, she wondered if people knew her ancestry. People in power. Maybe that's why she lived in the mud while they lived in real houses.

She pushed all these thoughts away while waiting with Emma and five other people in a small cubed area blocked off by black curtains. She began clearing her mind for whatever awaited her on the other side of the barrier. Rather than being led through the curtain, someone started talking to them from the other side of it.

"Are you prepared to pledge your support to The Voiceless Pure?"

"Yes," was the enthusiastic response around her. Feeling a little uneasy, she wondered if that was the name of the group that had hosted the protest, but Emma seemed to know what was happening.

"Repeat the oath after me. As one of The Voiceless Pure…. I will agree to take orders…. and use my powers… for the good of the group… and the benefit of the Tuatha Dé Danann."

She murmured the words along with her fellow new members during the pauses, but her uneasiness grew. It seemed like a lot to promise. The support she'd had in mind had been more about voting for them when they all became adults or maybe attending more protests. Hazel considered backing out, but Emma's eyes were shining, and their hands were still clasped. Besides, technically she'd already said the oath.

Deciding to go all in with Emma, she didn't even mind when the following words floated over from the other side of the curtain. "Do you agree to a punishment by your peers if you ever break the secrets of The Voiceless Pure?"

This time she was ready and added a "Yeah" to the chorus of agreements.

A hand pushed through a handful of brown armbands. "Put one of these symbols on and come through the shield one at a time for greeting."

When only the two of them remained, Emma pushed Hazel through with a big smile, following right behind her. "We stick together," she told the startled man on the other side. Hazel was alarmed. He was an adult, the first she'd seen participating, but she supposed someone older must be in charge of helping organize things.

She only had a moment to note that his armband was green when he waved them on through another curtain. On the other side was the same meeting room Hazel had been in the last time. There were a lot fewer people chatting in small groups, and the stage was empty.

"Hello," a familiar voice said. In front of them was the speaker from the other night. Still in jeans, with a different colored crop top today, her bright blue armband was prominently displayed.

"Ariana!" Emma squealed and squeezed Hazel's hand tight. "I'm such a big fan."

Hazel tried not to feel jealous of Emma's attention to the older girl. Instead, she wondered how and where Emma could have become a big fan and not told her best friend about it until now.

"Your first task is one of information," said Ariana. "We need people to know what's going on. The two of you should visit as many clans as possible to explain that MacLir is working with the humans to keep us in these caves. Returning to our golden era is possible, but MacLir must be stopped first."

The girls nodded. Although it was the first time, Hazel heard that MacLir was involved. Her father had made strange comments about the sea god when drunk. Was this what he'd been referring to?

"Do either of you have developed powers yet?"

After Emma gushed about her hypnotism, Hazel said shyly that she could move things.

"Ah, another kinetic," said Ariana.

"Actually, no," said Emma, "much better. She can transport things. If she's been to both places or shown a map and picture, she can send items to all kinds of places."

"Only non-living things, though," Hazel pointed out quickly. People always asked next if she could transport people that way, but it never worked.

Ariana's eyes lit up, and she said, "After your travels through the caves spreading the message, come back here this time next week. We are forming a special group I think the two of you would be perfect for."

CHAPTER 5

Clara

"It won't change me, will it? I like me the way I am," said Clara.

"Wouldn't you wish to have an easier time in the world?" Piper's hand stilled while petting her kitten Flutter, her unbound hair sliding sideways in a confused head tilt that reminded Clara of a pigeon.

"Of course I do, but the world needs to change its views and learn to accept differences. I got tired of trying to change myself to fit their mold a long time ago. I've learned to appreciate how my brain works and would not lose that for any amount of magic."

Piper nodded, quietly considering her words as she left Clara alone to change into the plain white dress. Ceremony day. It felt like it had come too quickly, but they told her the waning moon was the best time, and better to do it now than to wait another month.

They'd picked up a group of elderly women in Dublin, all at least a couple decades older, which made her feel both old and young. Even though she looked younger than these women, she felt as old as them and was about to become a sage like they were.

Piper had ushered her to change clothes while the others got off the ship and began preparations. Only Lucky remained when she came back out on the deck, and he simply pointed to the rope ladder.

When she set foot on a quiet, empty beach at the bottom of a cliff, impossible to reach without a ship, Wave Sweeper moved out into the water a reasonable distance away.

All the women were waiting patiently in a group, chatting. The scene seemed so normal. The sound and smell of the sea were calming, and the last of Clara's worries slipped away, replaced with enthusiasm. She was going to become a goddess. She was ready.

Brigit glanced at the sun low in the sky as it created a streak of orange on the horizon that faded to darker blues the higher the light traveled. The sun swiftly disappeared from view, and as the beach plunged into twilight, she said, "Let it begin."

The older women slowly moved until they stood in a line close to Clara. Piper and Amy had both worn their ceremonial goddess dresses and moved back out of view.

"Pixies!" Brigit called out, and a cloud of them seemed to blow down from the top of the cliff.

Thin naked bodies with huge black eyes swarmed closer, and she heard a buzz filling the breezy sea air from their iridescent bee-shaped wings. They flitted so fast it was hard to see them until they separated and perched in the hair of the elderly women, causing one of the old ladies to giggle.

"These sages have gathered to impart their important words to Ireland's next goddess of wisdom. Begin." Brigit clapped her hands.

The pixies sprang up as the first woman spoke and began circling her. She was the tallest and nearly wrinkle-free, with a pretty, open face and a big grin. "Make someone smile at least once a day." As she spoke in her Swedish accent, the pixies drew dark metallic silver from her and then moved on down the row, doing the same for each one.

The next was a portly woman, and she said in a thick Scottish brogue. "The path to failure is tryin' to please everyone."

An Asian sage was third in line, her dark eyes shining from a cheery round face full of wrinkles. In heavily accented English, she said, "The pain in life lets us welcome the joy in life."

The pixies finished with her and moved on to a black woman who was at least in her nineties and probably from America, judging by her accent, who said, "Never dwell on life's troubles. Think of the good times."

Last was a large Samoan, the youngest of the group. "Don't worry about things you can't do anything about," she said with an easy smile and a wink.

The pixies were nearly invisible in the cloud of silver magic they carried. Then, finally, Amy appeared at the edge of Clara's vision holding a large wooden bowl full of blueberries. She tossed it over Clara's head, saying, "To always remain sweet."

Before a single blueberry could hit the sand, they were absorbed into the silver cloud of pixies. Then, starting at the bottom near her feet, they wove the two items into the white dress, turning it into a deep midnight blue color with a hint of dark silver. Finally, they finished with the sleeves, and all landed in her hair to wait, each one clutching a few strands.

Brigit stepped forward with a handful of coins. She tossed them in the air in front of Clara, saying, "Be both hard and malleable in the face of hardship." The fairies let the coins drop, but before they touched the sand, a glowing metallic gold color was pulled from them.

Piper stood across from Brigit, holding another wooden bowl filled with tiny chips of diamonds. "Be the shining star in people's lives," she said as sparkling diamonds showered around Clara. The pixies caught them inside the gold cloud and began weaving, starting with her hair.

As the last of the diamonds disappeared from their pixie cloud, a breeze blew in, and they let it blow them all away. The wind continued to flurry around the small beach but only seemed to affect Clara. Her dress blew and flapped in the gale while not a hair on anyone else even shifted.

The cloudless storm carried crackly energy that centered around her. The wind disappeared as quickly as it had picked up. She felt tingly all over when the energy wrapped around her like a cocoon. It poured into her as if she'd taken the magic into her lungs instead of air. For one instant, she felt the island. It wasn't only something under her feet. It was a living thing. In the air and under the sea. In every tree and pebble. The feeling faded, and she could breathe again.

Her new midnight blue dress with a marbling of gold had a fitted high top and long loose sleeves ending in cuffs. The sensible skirt flowed down and flared out for easy walking. The sparkly diamond chips were spread in a random pattern all over the dress, with a touch of permanent gold and diamond sparkle added to her hair.

With the ceremony over, they dropped the human sages off at a Dublin pub, then settled on the new ship benches. Besides the bench extensions, another new addition to the ship was the string lights hanging from the mast to add a festive glow. Yet, instead of feeling merry, everyone was quiet while Lucky flew Wave Sweeper back to sea.

Darkness fully descended when Clara had her first vision. A scene passed in front of Clara's eyes. It only took seconds, then she turned to Lucky and said, "It is foolish being obsessed with past failures." Lucky raised an eyebrow at her but said nothing as he continued to concentrate on guiding the ship.

"What was that about?" Amy asked.

"I think that was my first magic! I had a vision of me telling that to Lucky. I guess he needed to hear it."

"So your power is much like mine. As a goddess of love, I play matchmaker. I see where and when people need to meet, then make it happen. As goddess of wisdom, you are a wise woman. You see what they need to hear, then tell them. I think Amy is the only one of the three of us that does powerful magic with her strength of mind."

"Absolutely," Clara agreed, nodding.

Amy blushed with a mixture of satisfaction and embarrassment but smiled at the compliment.

Piper

Brigit had mentioned how the three of them could be linked after Clara's ceremony as the crone. The other night Piper felt during dinner that they were all family. She wanted that forever. That connection and sense of family. For herself and for her daughter.

"Brigit," began Piper, "now that Clara has crone magic, how do we combine the magic? I remember you saying it was possible."

Brigit glanced at Lucky and then said, "Two ways are possible. First, like a marriage, you can announce it and spend time together. You will eventually become closer, and your magics could intertwine a bit. Or, well…"

Piper wondered if Brigit looked uncomfortable, but couldn't be sure. She waited as patiently as possible, but when the other woman failed to continue, Piper prompted her, saying, "Or, what?"

"Blood magic is out of fashion but would be the strongest. Not all of it is bad. Nothing is good or bad, really. It's how the magic is used."

Lucky frowned.

"What would that do?" Clara asked.

"Link the three of you forever. It can't be undone. However, all your powers would be stronger, and you'd potentially gain some small side magic as a benefit."

"Let's do it!" Piper announced. She'd had an uneasy feeling all year that worse things were on the horizon for everyone connected to the fairy mounds. MacLir especially. She'd overheard him talking to Robin and Lucky about war possibly brewing. After the attack in the tunnels, it seemed likely. They would need all the help they could gather, even if it came from themselves. Amy and Clara nodded. Hesitantly, but agreeing.

"Take us to The Hill of Tara," Brigit announced.

Lucky frowned again, but the ship turned. The sails billowed out in the opposite direction.

"Blood magic is safer at sacred sites. The Hill of Tara was where the Tuatha Dé Danann ruled from when we were in power. We don't have to go near the touristy bits. Being on the hill will be enough."

The silence returned, but that was fine with Piper. She preferred quiet. Vixen padded out of the cabin, and Piper slid down to the polished deck to join her. The large dog flopped down her tired old bones into a regal sitting position close to Piper's thigh, her petite paws in front of her.

"They are asleep," said Vixen. "MacLir and the baby both fell asleep on the bed after eating."

"I'm glad," sent Piper, "they both need the rest. Is Emily doing well?"

"She is not so hot to touch. I believe she'll be fine. Children get sick, but it passes."

Piper had been a little worried about Emily's first cold, but the symptoms were fading as soon as they came. She was glad Vixen and MacLir could watch over her daughter while she was busy tonight.

"As for protection, a huge sea creature has been hanging around the ship when we are in the water."

Piper wondered if the dog meant Fia. Although, she hadn't seen the sea dragon in weeks. Long before Vixen came to live on the ship. She wondered if the old dog's senses were failing but decided it might be one of those times to not point out tidbits like that.

She reassured the dog as the ship landed with a thump. As soon as it was down, Lucky let loose with everything he could not say while concentrating on flying. "I'm not sure this is a good idea. Blood magic? Really, Brigit? I didn't even know you knew how. Where's MacLir? I think we should consult him first before we do anything. It's already unnatural that humans have magic through Tua De ceremonies. Worse to bind them further to the island with blood."

"Humans aren't allowed to have magic? Since when? You sound like The Voiceless Pure." The last sentence Brigit spoke had the effect of a slap to Lucky. He snapped his mouth shut, his eyes going dark green in anger.

"Times have changed," Brigit continued. "I may not have a great love for all humans, but I do care about our friends. I have a feeling this is the right path. I'm trusting my instincts. You should trust me too."

Lucky looked away, breathing deeply for a few moments. "I still don't agree, but I won't stop you." Then, standing, he touched foreheads with Brigit as a silent apology for his outburst, then marched off to the cabin with tense shoulders.

"Don't mind him. This is not only big magic. It's women's magic. Something the High Court has been trying to suppress since, well, since it first formed. We rarely did big magic even at our height of power, and never these days." Next, Brigit explained the words and actions to accompany the spell, adding, "Good luck."

"What do you mean good luck?" asked Clara. "Aren't you coming with us?"

"No, this bond is between the three of you. Only you can be present, or it could taint the magic."

Piper finally hesitated. Everything was suddenly more alarming than when Brigit first talked about it. Maybe she should rouse MacLir first and speak to him. Although that would wake up the baby. Besides, Brigit wouldn't let them do anything dangerous, and Piper's newly awakened instincts also pointed her in this direction.

Walking under the waning moonlight, she glanced back at Brigit, standing tall at the ship's edge and waving solemnly. Piper waved back, then focused on finding her footing on the grassy hill and the task ahead.

"I think right here should be good enough," said Clara after a ten-minute hike upward. She stopped them at a high point on the hill. They could see in all directions, and the ship was lost to the darkness below them. Standing in a loose circle and holding hands, she said clearly, "Let it begin."

With Piper's tiny pocket knife, they each made a cut on their thumb. Then, careful not to let anything drop too soon, they pressed all three thumbs together and let the mingled blood drip into the soil below.

For a heartbeat, nothing happened, and with a twinge of relief, Piper wondered if they did it wrong. Or, maybe the big magic Brigit talked about didn't work for humans. Although, as a goddess already tied to nature, was she still completely human? She felt something, a stirring of power, a crackle of electricity. It started deep inside her and pushed outward.

The electric feeling shot out of her feet and burned a circle of light in the grass around her. The same was happening to the others. After the light burned the single ring around each of them, it spiraled like a burner on a stovetop. Finally, all three spirals joined the other circles to form an interconnected triple spiral shape.

Three small balls of light bounced up from the space in the center of the triple spiral and floated up to hover over their heads. The glow dimmed enough to see that each light wasn't merely a ball but a phase of the moon. A waxing half-moon shone over Piper and a waning half-moon over Clara, with a full moon over Amy.

Their moons spun a moment, then floated down. Clara held out her hand first, palm up. The action reminded Amy and Piper of Brigit's instructions to do the same. The fist-sized ball of light, showing the waxing moon, landed in Piper's hand. It was faintly warm. At Clara's nod, all three closed their hands over the light. It vanished, absorbed into Piper's skin, setting off a wave of warmth starting at her fingertips and spreading through her body.

The crackling energy of her first ceremony returned. It was different, though. Stronger this time, like she'd touched a hundred electrically charged door knobs at once. She felt the shock. It raced through her body, around the spiral shape at her feet, and then further. In her mind, she could see the lines burning a thin line outward through the grass, across sidewalks and streets, to show every channel of power in Ireland.

She could see them all in a vision that flowed into her mind for a moment. As if she was above Ireland. The island was lit with a web of crisscrossed lines leading into the surrounding ocean before fading off.

Then the power retracted, racing back to Tara. It rushed into the spiral at their feet before abandoning the circle to flow up through the three women. There the power settled, and all was calm.

"What in the world," said Amy.

Piper didn't hear the words with her ears. Instead, they dripped into her mind, exactly like how she spoke with Vixen, Flutter, and other animals she'd chatted with. It was something she knew how to do. Pushing the words toward Amy, she sent, "Don't think too loud. I can hear you."

Amy jumped and glanced over at Piper. "You can hear my thoughts?" The sending was loud and drove Piper to her knees with hands over her ears. Though logically, she knew that would do no good.

Joining in, Clara thought, "Are we speaking mind-to-mind?"

"Not so strong," Piper sent toward them. "Quietly, please."

"Sorry," Amy said aloud, "but can you hear every thought or only what I send? Can you hear this?"

Piper braced for another painful sending, but nothing happened. "No. If you are thinking right now, I can't hear it. The first one must have slipped through by accident. It gets easier as you practice."

The walk down the hill was a more treacherous, the moonlight only helping a little. At one point, Clara muttered, "I wonder." They paused to watch her hold out her hand, and the waning moon appeared. The glowing ball of light illuminated the ground around her feet.

Excited to try, Piper remembered the feeling of the light in her palm, the soft warmth and calm it brought with it. When she opened her fist, the light was there, her waxing moon. She closed her palm, wishing it away, and it was gone. Then opened her palm while remembering it there, and it reappeared.

Amy's full moon lit up the beaming smile on her face. Delighted, they used their new power to navigate the rough terrain of the hill.

When the ship came into view, they could noticed Brigit watching for their return. So, she was the first to see the bright new triple goddess. Maiden in pale blue, Mother in summer green, and crone in midnight blue. Three stages of womanhood in three women, but one connected magical being.

CHAPTER
6

Hazel

"I've been worried sick," hissed a voice behind her.

Fingers dug into Hazel's arm, forcing her to drop the plate she was filling with food. The hand swung her around, and her mother's glaring eyes were inches from hers.

Too startled to resist, she only had time for a backward glance at Emma, who shrugged at parental problems. Hazel shrugged back, and Emma's mouth twisted into a rueful smile.

In moments they were in an empty hallway of the great hall where the daily feast was being served. Her mother had not let go of the death grip on her arm. As if the old woman thought Hazel would poof away if not held in place.

Her mother glared, waiting for Hazel to show fear, simper, and apologize like always. Instead, she rolled her eyes, then stared back. Hazel wasn't playing the game this time and watched that realization appear in her mother's eyes.

Trying to regain the upper hand, her mother repeated, "I've been worried sick." She followed this statement with a teeth-rattling shake. The movement caused pain to shoot up Hazel's arm, where her mom's firm grip would surely leave bruises. Hazel ignored it, leaving her face passive, but rolling her eyes again simply because she knew it would irritate her mother. "You've been gone for weeks," her mother added. When anger and rabid shaking failed a second time, she let go of Hazel and took a step back.

Hazel noted that she could see the top of her mother's head as she did. She'd grown taller, yet she'd feared this woman? One corner of her mind still clung to that fear. No longer, she told that part of herself. "Do you need something?" Hazel asked in the most uninterested voice she could manage.

Her mother gasped. Probably at the disrespect in her tone, Hazel thought with glee. Being with Emma had boosted her confidence. Joining the Voiceless Pure had given her life purpose. Now this new ability to unnerve her mother for once? This was true power.

Scrambling to assert control, her mother said, "Yes, I need something. I need you to come home right now."

"And miss the feast? Aren't you the one always saying how important the meal is? How we must be seen participating. Well, here I am. Participating. So, what's your objection?"

"Why are you wearing that ridiculous armband?" Changing the subject was one of her mother's favorite weapons, but she'd picked the wrong topic this time.

"Because I'm one of The Voiceless Pure," Hazel said with her chest puffed out and chin up. The newest dress she'd stolen was a little warmer, with long sleeves, and worn with leggings. Red and fitted, her mother wasn't there to comment on how it clashed with her coloring or that she was too chubby for something so tight. Instead, the blue armband wrapped around her upper arm gave her a flush of pride every time she caught a glimpse of it out of the corner of her eye.

"This is a blue armband. Everyone starts with brown, but I moved up quickly because I was selected to join a special group. I'm valued. There." Her emphasis on the last word was meant to show that she had been undervalued elsewhere.

Her mother caught the implied slight, and her eyes narrowed. "You are valued at home. Your grandmama misses you."

Hazel snorted. "Misses me waiting on her every whim, you mean? Pass. I'm doing real work now. I'm spreading the message and creating change. We are changing our future!"

Her mother's anger faded into a deep frown. "What message?" she asked.

"Did you know MacLir is holding us down in these tunnels? He's joined the humans against us."

"Poppycock. He's done nothing except help us. Don't you remember the bedtime stories I used to tell you about him when you were little?"

"It turns out they were wrong. All of them! So, if we can remove him from power, we can live above ground again. Return to a golden era." Remembering her daydream of the house with wood floors and many windows, Hazel could not help the smile that spread across her face.

Her smile vanished when her mother laughed. Loud and hard. The burst of mirth echoed down the hall and nearly bent the woman double. "You joined a cult," she said as she wiped the water from her eyes. "You've let people get their claws into you, and now you don't know up from down, do you?"

Color rose in Hazel's cheeks, and shame tried to swamp her. The challenge in her mother's tone and a smug smile brought back that tiny part of her that still feared her mother's opinion. Hazel mentally crushed that part of her. Squished it flat, then tore it into little pieces. Her mother had gone too far, and any feelings she had that they might one day resolve their differences were gone for good.

Trying not to cry from the surge of emotions coursing through her, she focused on her mother and the negativity her presence brought to Hazel's life. She pinned the woman in place with the angriest glare she could muster. "I'm not coming home. Ever." She stalked away, her shoulders tense. Braced for her mother to try something to detain her.

She desperately wanted to look back to see if her mother would follow but refused to give her the satisfaction of knowing how badly that laugh had hurt. That one, and all the ones before it, when Hazel had shared her dreams of the future.

She'd been upset at her parents working in the kitchens instead of having captured humans for labor. In the new future, she had planned to help them resettle above ground with a house and a maid for grandmama. It would be easy to get free servants like she got free clothes. She remembered the store clerk and how easily controlled humans were.

Apparently, humans were useful back in the golden era. Her assigned group of other blue bands had reasoned that if they were returning to a golden era, that must mean having humans cook and clean again. Everyone in her group agreed the humans were dumb but would make good servants.

Everything must have been wonderful when Tuatha Dé Danann ruled Ireland. It was unfair that she'd had to grow up underground in the first place. She should always have lived in a seasonal landscape with sunlight on her face and arms. Soon she could be there with Emma, enjoying the seasons together. Maybe getting a house together.

With a shudder, she realized that if the movement's plans for change didn't work, the only home she had was her parent's cave. She'd never have a way to move out to her own place because no more unoccupied space existed underground. She'd have to live with her mother forever. That was not an option.

The Voiceless Pure had plans for change, and she was helping spread the message. All these daily conversations for spreading awareness would work, and the laws would be changed. She was sure of it.

Clara

The warm breeze and white sands eased a tense feeling in her chest that she hadn't known were there. Shaking out a blanket, Clara lay in the shade of a palm tree and rested her eyes. The shush of the waves was broken only by the occasional louder chatter of Piper and Amy further down the beach.

Clara smiled at their happy gossipy tones and was glad they were no longer discussing the dangers of the tunnels in Ireland. Such a serious conversation ended them here in this peaceful place, where she was delighted to take a break from the worries of her new home. However, she still shuddered when remembering the worst bit of news that the magical community wanted war with the humans.

The warmth and waves began to lull her to sleep, yet the memory from a few days ago floated into her mind as her eyes closed. Everyone squished onto the newly widened ship seats as Lucky outlined all the reports he was hearing. "It's bad. They've reached every clan with lies, turning every Tua De angry about the humans. But even angrier at MacLir for causing the problem in the first place and holding them underground."

MacLir's eyebrows had snapped together, and he'd opened his mouth to protest, but Piper put a reassuring hand on his arm while Lucky waved him to silence, saying, "Enough, MacLir. Of course, we all know you did nothing. Repeating it to us won't help. The High Court, for whatever reason, has maintained the laws about not leaving the mounds. Strangely, that is a part of the message the rebels are using, but twisting it, so it sounds like the High Court must get your approval to leave, and you are refusing to give it."

Amy had snorted at the idea, and Brigit shook her head at her people's ignorance. Both sobered at the next word.

"War," said Lucky. "That's what they are agitating the people toward. They want control of the human realm in Ireland."

The group had sat in silence for several moments, which made Fia's appearance all the more startling. The dragon's head shot up out of the water and pushed in close to the conversation. Piper jumped in her seat, and Clara's heart started to drum.

If the beast could smile, it would have been. Clara imagined it having an elbow to lean on with a smug smile. "Why don't you get away for a while?" Fia explained they had met Piper in much warmer waters than these and that they often swam in those calmer Caribbean waters before adding, "Maybe time for a vacation?"

Lucky was the first to agree, pointing out that MacLir's presence was only causing more issues, plus it was getting dangerous for Brigit as a known ally. Maybe shifting away from the situation would give the mounds time to calm down. The new triple goddess, Piper, Amy, and Clara, agreed a break from the danger might be what everyone needed. Although privately, Clara considered it might quickly get much worse without their input rather than better. Then, MacLir admitted he wanted to do some treasure hunting, so here they were.

Clara had never enjoyed the relentless heat in her desert home, but this lovely drowse-inducing warm breeze had a whiff of salt water. The sound of Amy's bright laughter woke her a little, and her busy mind refused to settle and let sleep take her. Instead, she thought about her new magic powers.

For the first few days, she could not help seeing the visions, but now she had better control over them. She saw both what she needed to say and the person's reaction. She was happy to share their helpful message with anyone with a positive response. For example, she told a young woman walking in the park, "It may not work out, but if you don't even try, it will surely fail." The woman's shoulders relaxed, and she thanked Clara before hurrying away.

Negative reactions were not appreciated. She chose not to deliver a message to the stocky middle-aged man dressed in a black suit standing in line behind her at the store. She could have told him in her vision, "When you judge something, you only prove that you have an incomplete view of it." In her second vision, he'd slapped her. So, she didn't feel like sharing that communication.

The visions helped her know what to say. However, they were also an added layer of exhaustion to every human interaction, which had already been distressing. Luckily, not everyone needed to hear something, and she rarely saw advice for her new family. She found that in addition to seeing visions at random times, she could usually see what guidance to give if she was asked.

"It's time for some treasure hunting! Who is going with me?" MacLir's voice boomed across the quiet, making Clara's eyes snap open. Giving up on a nap, she moved closer to see what the commotion was about.

MacLir leaned over and jiggled the hand of his infant daughter, who smiled up at him. "Can someone watch Emily while Piper swims with me?"

Piper shifted in her folding beach chair and said nothing. However, through their new bond, Clara could pick up the deep discomfort she was feeling. Mostly, they'd found they could all keep thoughts to themselves after the linking ceremony. Unless it was a strong emotion. It reminded her of how the world said autistic people didn't feel emotion, but it was often the opposite. She felt it so deeply that she had to keep a tight hold on it like she could feel Piper doing now.

The excited light in MacLir's eyes dimmed when Piper whispered, "I'd prefer to stay on the beach." Clara could see the hurt MacLir was feeling. Years of practice, added to motherhood, had brought her to an understanding of how to see when others were upset. It also helped that Piper had confided in her that MacLir was desperate to get her in the water, and she was equally desperate not to go.

Hoping to diffuse the situation, Clara stepped forward and said, "I'd love to go, MacLir. Maybe Piper can go another time when she feels more up to it."

Amy jumped in, adding she'd also love to go see underwater and look for treasure. Eager participants eased the sadness in MacLir's eyes. He leaned down, kissed Piper and Emily, and then led the treasure-hunting expedition down the beach.

Clara felt a sending come into her mind from Amy, "Do you think Piper will be okay alone while we are gone?"

"You asked that too loud, Amy. I can hear you," came Piper's mildly annoying voice next. Amy's ears reddened to have been overheard. She was still the worst at directed sending in their group.

Clara chuckled and sent to both of them, "I believe Piper is capable. Besides, where did Brigit and Lucky get off to?"

"They went on an exploration of the island." A satisfied overtone infused the sending, showing the goddess of love approved. Although Clara never planned to fall in love again, watching the older couple discover each other was sweet. Seeing some happiness in the world was nice, especially a second chance at love.

She knew Lucky and Brigit were much older than she was but felt some kinship with them as, in appearance, the three of them were the oldest in the group. As such, she was surprised by their vacation clothes. While MacLir often wore shorts and nothing else, for this trip, Amy wore short shorts with a bikini top, while Lucky and Brigit were not clad in much more. Both were in shorts and thin tops to combat the tropical heat. Only Piper wore her usual stretchy black jeans and a blue tee shirt. Clara wondered if the thin summer dress she wore would suit their little undersea search.

When they reached the water, neither Clara nor Amy had any extra focus for continued musings. After handing each of them a knapsack, MacLir was already chest-deep in the water and not stopping. As if he expected them to walk directly into the waves with him.

She'd gotten about waist deep when Amy sent, "Perhaps treasure hunting is not a hobby I wish to start." At chest deep, Clara felt a similar hesitation to Amy. The clear sparkling aqua water, so enchanting moments ago, seemed menacing when facing disappearing under the surface of the vast expanse stretching out to the distant horizon. Protectiveness washed over her, even stronger than her excitement about sunken treasures. Amy was upset, and she'd always taken care of her sister. Making a choice to lead Amy back to the beach, Clara was frozen by seeing something large moving in the water near her feet.

Her strong imagination jumped to any number of possibilities and screamed when it shifted closer and grabbed both her ankles. She barely had time to take part of a breath before she was yanked under the water. Almost immediately, her face felt dry, as if she was not only still above the water, but her face and hair had never been wet in the first place.

She opened her eyes to see a bubble of air surrounding her head. Beyond the transparent bubble, she could see Amy's annoyed expression also surrounded by a bubble. MacLir's mischievous eyebrows high, he jerked his head toward the depths, took each by the hand, and dragged them down into the deep.

Speeding through the water, she caught glimpses of coral below them as fish darted out their way. The masts and rigging lines of an old ship loomed in the distance. Like Wave Sweeper, the sunken vessel tilted to one side with holes in the hull. A shark appeared from the ship's shadows, swimming at a lazy pace, indifferent to the fish darting in and out of the holes.

MacLir ignored all the sea creatures and led them into the nearest cavity. The filtered sunlight disappeared in the deep gloom. Clara guessed that MacLir could see in the dark better than she could. Holding out the hand not grasped by the sea god, she concentrated on the memory of warmth of her palm. The glowing waning moon appeared, and, as always, she felt a thrill run through her that she was capable of magic.

Amy's light appeared on MacLir's other side, and he looked from one shining moon to the other and smiled approvingly. Contrary to what Lucky had implied, MacLir didn't care the women had been linked as the triple goddess. Which made Clara wonder if it was simply Lucky's old-fashioned prejudice that had made him object to the female-only ceremony.

"What are we supposed to do now?" sent Amy.

"I wish we could ask MacLir," replied Clara. It soon became clear directions were not needed. MacLir released their hands, made sure they were both watching, and tossed a crate to the ground. It sank slowly, but the force MacLir used was enough to crack the weakened wood on impact. It broke apart, and MacLir sat among the scattered wreckage, happily sifting through it like a toddler playing with blocks.

Clara was game for more discovery, so she knocked over the nearest crate, which sent bags of small unknown objects bursting free. Then, realizing this could be a time-consuming search and potentially become dull, she glanced over to see if Amy was having better luck. Instead, came face to face with Fia.

The sea dragon had seemed large next to the ship during their first meeting, but up close in the water, it was clear the dragon was truly enormous. The bulk of their eel-like body still outside the ship was outlined in the sunlight filtering down in the depths.

Clara's little ball of light lit up the dragon's face and deep black shifting eyes. So, when Fia's mouth opened, Clara got a distressingly clear view of the dragon's rows of teeth and fangs as long as her arm. The sea dragon clamped down on the edge of Clara's dress and wriggled back out of the ship dragging the new captive with them.

CHAPTER 7

Tamlin

The color caught his eye first. A bit of rich, dark green fabric peeked out from a scrap caught in a door. It drew him in, and Tamlin could not stop himself from opening the closet to see more. The tiny ship closet displayed the most magnificent wardrobe he'd ever seen.

Not just the green fabric attached to a long dress with a high split on one side but also a rainbow of colors in all his favorite hues and fabrics. The owner of these clothes had already been led away, but he wished he could have known the human who had gathered these extraordinary clothes. He felt they might have been friends.

The heavy canvas of his white jumpsuit uniform scraped along his arm as he reached out thin, delicate fingers to stroke the smooth fabric of a sapphire blue shirt. The satin was attractively overlaid with sequin-encrusted lace across the shoulders and upper sleeves.

A thrill of satisfaction ran through him from knowing what each of the fabrics and embellishments was named. He'd learned it all from a book stashed in his private room, where he'd poured over the pages exploring the use of different fabrics in fashion.

The book was where he'd learned the fabric he'd worn all his life was called canvas. For the longest time, he'd thought canvas was simply another word meaning ship sails, which is where his current outfit's fabric had been cut from, but it turned out humans wore canvas on purpose as part of regular clothing. The collar of the jumpsuit rubbed roughly against his neck, and, not for the first time, he resolved that if it was up to him, he'd never wear the material again.

He didn't think it was his foster father's idea to wear identical clothes. Instead, one of his father's generals pointed out that the leaders should match. When he'd asked his father why, the man had mumbled something about tradition and refused to say more.

Remembering his father caused a confused twinge in Tamlin's chest. A mixed-up swirl of emotions he tried to avoid. Love for the man, sadness for his semi-recent death, anger at his betrayal of Ian, discomfort at his ideals, dread at having to take his place as High King.

Tamlin had never wanted to be king. Never. He stroked some yellow chiffon and dreamed instead of designing his own clothes. Many clothes brought in over the years had caught his eye, but this one was especially charming. He imagined the soft fabric sliding on his skin, the fluttering sleeves tickling his shoulders. It was just his size too, and the high waistline would look excellent on his slim frame.

Yellow was not a color that would look good with his flawless creamy pale skin, but he couldn't resist. "You shall be mine," he told the fabric, pulling the dress from its hanger and bundling it into a nearby bag, packing it as best as he could to avoid creasing it.

Noticing extra room in his over-the-shoulder bag, he quickly decided to take the green dress too. The forest hue gave him happy chills when he looked at it. Its silky fabric intrigued him too much to leave it behind. He'd never been to a forest in person, but he imagined the dress's texture was how dark green summer leaves would feel.

He was folding in the last drape of fabric when he heard a footstep behind him.

"Why are you gathering clothes, sir?" Tamlin's second in command stood in the doorway of the ship's cabin. His eyes were trained on the bag of dresses.

Tamlin panicked. No one had ever questioned why he insisted on checking out captured ships first. He was the new king; he could do as he wanted. No one had disobeyed his orders to stay off the ship until he was done, so this was the first time he'd been caught salvaging clothes. "They are for the, uh… recent arrivals."

"Captives are always issued clothes at their assigned stations," pointed out his second in command. Sam. He wasn't supposed to know the man's name since they were not family, but his assigned assistant was so helpful and kind. They were almost friends, and it didn't feel right not knowing his name. So when no one looked, he'd snuck into the records and found the name. Although, it was difficult not to use it now that he knew it.

"True. True." He tried not to appear nervous, stalling for time to find a good reason for pilfering clothes from the wrecked ship. Luckily, thinking on his feet was one of his strong points. "These are to comfort the captives for the first few days, in case they are homesick."

His second's posture relaxed, and his lips parted in a beautiful smile. "You are always so kind, sir." The words made Tamlin feel a little floaty for some reason, more so when his companion reached out to lay a hand over Tamlin's.

At the gentle touch, warmth raced up Tamlin's arm like flames licking up from the base of a curtain. Curiously, he noted the fire was spreading through the rest of him and making him a little lightheaded. He didn't pull away.

Tamlin once felt this way in the physician's wing, warm and lightheaded during healing. Could his second be sending him healing without realizing it? "Uh, remind me, what born magic do you have?"

"Speaking with animals, sir," said Sam, almost reluctantly pulling his hand back and returning to the doorway.

"Right. Yes," agreed Tamlin. He remembered now. So, the fiery warmth he'd felt was not fire magic or healing magic.

"I came to let you know the sea dragon has notified us that the prisoners will arrive soon. I've put preparations in place, but you should make yourself available and stay near the north wing if possible. In the meantime, I'll leave you to your... ship inspection." The man's eyes gleamed in an expression that Tamlin could not identify, then he was gone.

Forgetting about creases, Tamlin hurriedly closed the bag to race both dresses back to his quarters. His prominent green armband always caught attention through the tunnels, as it was stitched with knotwork designs to signify the position of the High King. So, on the way, he nodded to underlings who stopped what they were doing to bow as he passed.

"We are changing our future!" he'd say as a greeting.

"We need to destroy all humans!" A younger man said with a fist raised. Tamlin understood the necessity of it but was always vaguely uncomfortable with the notion. Admittedly there were too many humans, but if all of them were destroyed, who would make silk? The queen of fabrics. He didn't want to live in a world without silk.

"MacLir has held us in the dark for too long!" One elderly man replied to his greeting. This was a sentiment Tamlin could wholeheartedly get behind. He could not imagine what kind of evil lived in the elemental that had forced generations of Tua De to live and die underground while humans enjoyed the earth.

At least they had the sea dragon's assistance. Cian had shown Tamlin how to control the beast in his role as High King. Fia had come in handy multiple times and was a crucial part of several of their plans. Especially the next one.

Clara

Being dragged to the surface by the dragon was faster than the descent with the sea god, and they were back on the island within moments. Above water, the magic bubble MacLir had provided for her popped, so Fia was careful not to dunk Clara in the water again. Dangling from their jaws by the hem of her dress, Clara was taken within viewing range of the island.

This was the opposite side of the island where they'd put the ship. Although even upside down and twirling, she could see Lucky and Brigit stretched in a shady bit of sand wrapped in each other's arms. The dragon opened their mouth to speak but lost hold of the dress, and Clara splashed into the water. She came upright again, sputtering and desperately treading to keep from going under again. Then, while trying to get the hair out of her eyes, she saw the dragon's face nearing.

"Stop! Stop right there. Don't you dare grab my dress again."

Fia froze. "You must come with me. You must."

"Not upside down!" Clara didn't love the idea of going anywhere with the dragon she didn't trust, but as long as they were talking, she wasn't getting dragged around with her underwear showing. "Can I follow you somewhere while on the ship?"

"No, no. Not ship." Fia's tail slapped the waves. The dragon's head ducked under the water, coming back up directly under Clara's legs. She had no choice but to cling to the neck of the sea dragon or fall back into the water. Actually, falling was still a concern, as the dragon was coated in a layer of slick slime. She reached out for something to steady herself and grabbed their ears. Fia shuddered but didn't object.

"You, you," shouted Fia.

Lucky sprang up from kissing Brigit, and his mouth dropped open on seeing Clara riding the dragon. "What are you doing up there?" Lucky called out across the water.

They were close to the island, but not close enough for Clara to think she could both jump off and then get safely on shore before the dragon nabbed her again. She was getting used to the slippery scales under her legs. She didn't want to accidentally be bitten in an escape attempt. Besides, MacLir would be along at any moment, and he would be able to fix things. Probably. Piper had once told her that everything in the sea loved and obeyed him, so Clara would wait patiently.

"Follow! Follow! Hurry," said Fia, mostly falling back into the water to swim around the other side of the island. They seemed to remember just in time not to completely submerge with a passenger on their back.

Hand in hand, Lucky and Brigit raced around the edge of the island toward the ship. MacLir and Amy appeared in the water, and Amy sent, "What's going on?"

"I'm not sure," Clara sent back, "the dragon is agitated and won't let me go. Can you ask MacLir to make it take me to the beach?"

She caught sight of Amy talking to MacLir, then they were out of visual range again. The dragon raced passed the ship to where Piper sat on the beach with Emily, but again stopped well before Clara could hope to escape.

"Piper, you must get up. Get up. Get up! Get on the ship. Hurry."

The panic in Fia's voice was different than anything the dragon had said so far, and actual worry fluttered in Clara's chest. "Fia, what's wrong?" She knew Fia could hear the question because she said it almost directly in the dragon's ears, but her words were ignored. Instead, Fia's eyes shifted wildly to take in MacLir approaching from the water and Lucky finally becoming visible on the beach.

MacLir's voice boomed out, "Fia, put Clara down. Right now."

Fia ignored the command as easily as Clara's question. "Get Piper on the ship. Hurry, hurry."

Amy's voice dripped into her mind, "MacLir says Fia is the one sea creature he can't control." Clara's heart dropped at the news. Now how would they make the dragon let her go? She reached out with her magic to see if the dragon needed to hear some advice, but the only thing the dragon needed to hear was, "Keep following your plan." Clara didn't share that, because it didn't seem like that would encourage the dragon to let her go.

Piper had been packing up the chairs and gear on the beach one-handed as Emily was sleeping on her other arm. MacLir called the ship over, and Lucky flashed everything on board as Piper climbed the ladder, and MacLir followed with Emily.

"Okay, we have Piper on board, as you asked. Now, release Clara," said MacLir. His usual soft boyish voice had a hard edge that Clara had never heard before.

"You, you. Get down," said the upset dragon, their tail slapping the water, alarm and haste still obvious in every word. "Only Piper and baby on the ship."

MacLir jumped from the deck, stomping back through shallow water to the island. Piper said, "Fia, we've done what you wanted, let Clara go."

"Follow me!" Fia shouted, shooting forward and pressing their body against the ship, pulling Wave Sweeper into the Otherworld's parallel realm. Clara saw the human side of the island shimmer, and the people on it disappeared from view. It only took moments for them to appear in the Otherworld. MacLir held hands with Amy and Lucky, who held Brigit's hand.

Fia had waited patiently for the four of them to get to the Otherworld, then said, "Piper must stay. The rest must follow." Fia gave Wave Sweeper a shove that sent the boat drifting away from the island in the opposite direction. "Come, come now, hurry."

Clara's sight was repeatedly blocked by Fia's large head and their erratic motions, but when Fia turned back to watch what the four on the beach were doing, she could see MacLir looking back and forth between his ship with its precious cargo and Clara being carted away by a sea dragon. Apparently, deciding Clara was in more danger, he dove into the water in the direction of the dragon.

"No!" Fia cried out, rushing back half the distance. Then, in the voice of a toddler on the edge of tears, they said, "All must come. Now. Not Piper. All others must follow me. Hurry!"

"Do you know what Fia wants?" Amy sent it to Clara and Piper.

"I have no idea," said Piper. Although her mental voice was faint with distance, as the ship continued to drift and she didn't stop it. Clara decided they should probably do some tests to see how far the sending would work but shelved the idea for a time when she wasn't kidnapped by a dragon.

"For now, stay on the ship and keep watch over Emily. Stay near the island, so we know where to find you later," sent Clara. Piper didn't reply, and Clara wondered if she had heard the message.

"We're coming," Amy sent. MacLir created bubbles around their heads, and in a hand-holding chain, they trailed him into the water, and he sped them toward the dragon, creating a wake like a speed boat.

Fia took off, staying far ahead but making it easy for the group to chase after Clara, who was carefully kept above the waterline. They were well out to sea now, not a piece of land in sight and Wave Sweeper long gone, when the dragon finally stopped.

"What is this about?" demanded MacLir when he was finally close enough.

"I'm sorry," said Fia.

CHAPTER 8

Clara

A noise came up out of the depths. A grinding of gears and screeching metal. A few feet away, the top of a dome surfaced. The paned glass dome was dark brown and covered in patches of algae growth. Clara felt drawn to it as if she wanted to jump off the dragon's back to get closer. Her mind was sluggish, yet it felt like the most important thing in the world to touch the dome. Everyone had a similar blank expression, which unnerved her as they were sucked through the glass and landed hard many feet below. Clara looked up and saw the faceted glass of the dome above. Littering the floor around them were unlucky dead sea creatures that had also fallen through the glass over time, creating an almost unbearable stench. "Where are we?"

MacLir stood and examined the odd space. "I thought I knew all the important places in both realms. I guess not."

Fia slithered like a snake to one side, coiling up as if trying to look small. Then, a door burst open on the far side of the dome, and eight men ran in to surround the group, yet completely ignored the sea dragon. They wore mismatched clothing from many eras and were all tall with brown hair and green eyes. They pointed various weapons at MacLir, from machine guns to crude spears.

Something about them seemed familiar, and they all wore brown armbands except for one, who wore a white jumpsuit and a blue armband. He was marginally taller than the others and surprisingly attractive in his baggy, shapeless clothing. He crooked a finger to one of his crew and pointed at Lucky. The man lept and landed on Lucky, knocking the air from his lungs. Another came forward with a big sturdy boot and stomped on his arm.

Lucky groaned as the bone snapped. The sound echoed loudly in the empty space. Brigit began to crawl toward him, but one of the crew blocked her way.

"Where is the flying ship?" Blue Armband demanded to know. "And I don't see the sea god's human mate here from the photos we were sent. You were ordered to bring everyone on that island. You failed, Fia."

The dragon's scales rippled and clacked, "Not fail. Piper girl was not on the island, and the flying ship was not in the given command."

Clara realized Fia was protective of Piper and had removed her from the island before following orders. For that reason, the group would probably forgive the dragon later. Although right now, they had bigger problems. They'd been trapped by people who knew everything about them, from their appearances to their weaknesses, like Lucky's inability to flash away when in pain.

Blue Armband sighed at the dragon but faced the group and announced, "It is my duty to inform you that you are now prisoners." MacLir slowly moved into a crouch, like a cat about to spring. "If you resist, we will shoot the women. So please slowly stand and walk through the doors to the processing area."

While the sea god hesitated, Clara cleared her throat to ask, "Would you at least tell me who we are prisoners of?"

Blue Armband proudly declared, "You are captives of a superior race! The pure Tuatha Dé Danann!"

They were led out of the dome, single file down four sets of broad and dimly-lit staircases with a guard between them so they could not communicate or plan. The stairs and tunnel walls were rough-cut stone, like sea caves, but very dry. Ahead of Clara, she could see Lucky cradling his arm, trying not to jostle it too much, and hoped Brigit could heal it soon.

At the bottom, they reached a medium-sized room lined with empty cages. Clara was baffled when they were not immediately jailed but instead lined up in chairs along one wall. The leader whispered to the crew, and one took off at a run. The rest of the captors stationed themselves around the room. Only Blue Armband stayed close enough to keep an eye on them.

"Why did you let us get taken?" Amy asked MacLir, shivering with a cold Clara felt but was trying to ignore.

"Those men have guns, and your immortality does not prevent death. Besides, I'm not invincible, you know." Amy looked as if she didn't know that, so MacLir added, "Well, I suppose the sea won't let me die, and if I were killed, I'd probably reappear on my island? The point is that the rest of you can be easily killed." Clara became aware that MacLir was staring at her as he said, "Clara, do you have any wise words for us?"

"I don't think I can do you as a group, so I'll have to find words for you individually." Then, starting with MacLir, she said, "Whoa, this is the most mysterious so far. Your advice is simply... don't. Do you know what that means?"

He grunted but nodded. "Yes. I was thinking of crashing the sea down to destroy this place because I could protect our group, but I guess I won't. I'll wait."

Preparing to do Amy next, Clara glanced over at the captors. She made eye contact with the leader, receiving his vision instead. "It's okay that you were listening to us. The important thing is to take the first step toward overcoming fear. It will give you the courage to make all your dreams a reality."

The Tua De moved closer, and keeping his voice low, he said, "How did you know…? I suppose it doesn't matter since it's true. I've long wanted it to end the atrocity that goes on here and… other things… but don't dare to act."

Deciding she could not keep thinking of the man as Blue Armband, Clara decided some introductions were in order. "MacLir, you seem to know, but this is Lucky and Brigit, also both Tua De. I'm Clara, and this is my sister Amy. What is your name?"

"I'm Sam," said the man with a lopsided smile. "Oh, and sorry about the arm, Lucky. I was following orders."

MacLir leaned forward. "Sam, could you tell us where we are?"

Sam looked around at the other guards and sighed. Still keeping his voice so low it could not carry, he explained, "You are a lot calmer than most newly caught folk, but I suppose you have all the same questions. Brace yourselves. You have discovered the secret of the Bermuda Triangle, and you will never see sunlight again. You are in the underwater kingdom of the Tuatha Dé Danann. We live comfortably here on stolen goods, served by humans captured through our attracting stations. This is a small ship-only station in the north wing, but some are big enough to suck in whole planes. I'm sorry to tell you, but like me, you will be stuck here for the rest of your lives. Only one person has ever left this place."

"Ian," Brigit said with a sigh of understanding.

Nodding, Sam said, "Yes, poor guy. Not that leaving did him any good."

Clara was hit with a second vision of the man. It was the first time she'd received two visions for one person in such a short time. "Hope is invincible. Hope changes everything. Have hope, Sam."

The Tua De leader began to back away, but a gleam came into his eyes that Clara thought might be hope or, instead, a reaction to the man striding into the room.

All the guards stood attentively when the new man entered. Obviously, a leader, the slim man in a white jumpsuit, marched straight up to Sam and stood tall next to him, glaring at their group. His broad forehead crinkled, and cupid's bow lips twisted into a deep frown. His thick wavy brown hair and eyebrows contrasted his flawless creamy pale skin, making his bright leaf green eyes stand out even in the dim lighting.

The embroidery on the man's armband was not something Clara had seen on anyone else. She wondered at the significance of it.

"Our people brought stronger magic to the human world, and we deserve to live where we please. We have you captured now, so this is the beginning of the end." Near the end of his speech, he focused on MacLir, and his frown had turned into a smug smile, which worried Clara more.

"Browns," called out Sam, "take these women to the nursery. I'll take the broken one, and our High King will take charge of the sea god."

Clara let herself be prodded forward but glanced back at Sam as he watched them leave and was sure he winked at her. Was their nervous helper hopeful after all?

Hazel

Emma put a chip in her mouth and then fed one to Hazel, who giggled. They'd taken a week off from their duties with the Voiceless Pure to finally spend a whole day in the human realm, which was glorious. They'd been able to explore more of the city than ever before and had ended up in the mall for dinner. After the day of sunshine and joy, approved by her team leader, she almost had to hold back tears at the thought of returning underground, even to something so lovely as Emma's home.

She pushed the anxiety away, for now, determined to enjoy this moment, and hold it as a beautiful memory of the finish of a perfect day with Emma. However, the noisy television in the corner of the food court was impossible to ignore. Extra loud music blared out, and a woman behind a desk said, "Breaking news out of the United States. Aerial bombs were stolen out of secure American military bases around the world. It's unclear how it could have happened, and many governments are preparing for possible retaliation until the bombs are recovered."

"I'm done eating," said Emma, pulling Hazel's focus back to the table. "Let's steal a few more dresses, and then we'll head back to my room." The half smile on Emma's face tugged at Hazel's heart. She knew what that meant and realized the lovely meal would not be the finale of their perfect day.

Leaving the remains of their meal on the table for some human to clean up, Hazel took Emma's hand and led her back to the shops for one last raid before they closed. She loved how their flowy dresses brushed as they walked, as if even their clothes could not stop touching, and showed how much they were in love.

The next day, at their first team meeting after returning, she was appalled when handed a brown one-piece jumpsuit. "These are the new uniforms. They are required," said her team leader, emphasizing the word required. Holding the rough fabric at arm's length, she cut her eyes to Emma, wanting to share her dismay, but Emma was already halfway changed into the thing with a big smile. So much for showing off their new dresses.

As the last to start changing, Hazel was also the last to leave the changing room. Emma had left with one of the other members in a heated discussion about some piece of political text from over two hundred years ago. Hazel had never paid enough attention to their history to debate the laws at Emma's level, so she was happy to let others feel her girlfriend's wrath over the lawmaking.

Proudly snapping on her blue armband and heading down a tunnel to their assigned team room, she glanced down a hallway at the intersection of tunnels. Two green armband leaders were standing in an open doorway, chatting quietly. Beyond them was one of the large meeting halls packed with rows of bombs. When one of the leaders caught her looking, he hurriedly shut the door but continued his conversation.

She picked up her pace to join her group, but her mind was buzzing. The news story from the night before flashed into her mind. Aerial bombs. What was her political movement doing with such weapons? She wanted to talk to Emma. It didn't feel right. It didn't match the message they'd been working so hard to spread about getting the laws changed.

Arriving in the team common area, she was further shocked to see the furniture had all been pushed to the walls. Her team members practiced fighting stances under the guidance of teachers she'd never seen before. Emma ran up to her and tugged her into the line. "You're late, slow-poke. You missed the announcement. It's time to form battle teams! Isn't this so exciting?"

Unease crawled through her watching all her new friends line up to fight each other in the new matching outfits. She wanted to talk to Emma about it, but the teacher came over and gave them instructions on how to start.

Emma leaned forward with an exaggerated pretend arm chop to Hazel's shoulder, repeating, "This is so exciting! We're finally going to make real progress in retaking the world above. The day we had together yesterday could be ours forever. We finally have hope."

All the facts rearranged in Hazel's brain at this twist in perception. Getting the laws changed was the first step for her people, but obviously, they would have to fight the humans to get them under control. Then, of course, they needed to learn both politics and fighting. It all made sense now, even the stolen bombs.

Her good mood returning, she did a twirl with an even more exaggerated fighting chop at Emma, leaning in so far she stole a kiss. Emma laughed, and they settled into their first day of soldier practice. To change the future for their clans.

Clara

"Amy, don't forget we're in the Otherworld. So, be careful what you think about here," sent Clara as they were led down yet another long tunnel, with guards in front and behind them. These tunnels were wider and let the sisters walk side by side, with room for people traveling in the opposite direction to still edge by. Brigit walked behind them, worryingly quiet.

Amy paled but sent jokingly, "Is that some of your magic wisdom?"

"No, it's common sense," Clara remembered the stories she'd been told of Amy's erratic powers of belief when in the Otherworld realm. Whatever her sister truly believed would happen, from lining the underground tunnels with flowers to opening a portal to a black hole in the bathroom, even as far as disintegrating a man.

Clara was already protective of Sam and didn't want Amy destroying all the guards in one swoop. Besides, based on

Sam's almost whispered worries, she felt more people would agree. Also, he'd mentioned human captives. Who knew how many innocent people lived in the warren of tunnels that Amy could harm with a careless thought?

They were pushed through a doorway into a wallpapered hallway with many doors. The door slamming and locking behind them seemed like a signal, and women of all ages came pouring into the hallway to greet them.

"Welcome to the nursery. My name is Kathrine," said one woman near Clara's age. "You must be weary and confused from your time in the cages. Please, come sit down and tell us about yourselves."

The other women nodded encouragingly and stepped back to let them follow Kathrine through one of the first doors. They sat down on the only couch in the room and were handed cups of tea. Kathrine sat opposite them in a wingback armchair. She smiled pleasantly while the other women settled around them on the floor in a half circle, all trying to have a good view of the newcomers.

"My name is Clara. I was born in America but have become an Irish goddess of wisdom. This is Amy, my sister, a goddess of creativity, and Brigit, a goddess of healing. We arrived with Manannán, the god of the sea, and Lugh, the ancient Irish god of travelers. Lugh can flash anywhere, so I'm sure he and MacLir are planning a rescue as we speak."

Kathrine's smile froze, and she wrinkled her nose. "Either you are the most amazing person I've ever met, or you are stark raving mad. I'm leaning toward the second one."

Amy's mental laughter was evident in her sending. "Maybe you should have checked what to say first, Irish goddess of wisdom."

Cutting her eyes to her sister in silent retort before looking back to the other woman, Clara quickly used her ability to learn what Katherine needed to hear. "Worlds are colliding soon, and we will escape. Your son, Luke, survived the crash and still needs his mother. Join us in a revolt."

"You can't say things like that here! They listen to everything we say and make an example of people who resist," began Katherine in a rush, but it was too late. The guards that had escorted them burst into the room and dragged Clara to her feet. One punched her in the ribs while the other kicked her feet out from under her. She fell hard, hitting her ear on the coffee table, before being dragged out by her ankles, her thin dress rolling up around her waist.

They stopped dragging her as soon as they were outside the nursery. One guard relocked the door while the other helped her to her feet. Both stared sternly at her as they led her a short distance away and opened a new door. She hesitated to step into the dark, but they pushed her in and locked it behind her.

Clara jumped as a voice from the shadows called out, "Who's there?"

CHAPTER 9

Clara

Clara opened her hand full of light, her moon glowing gently in the center. It lit up Lucky's pained face, he was sitting in front of supply shelves.

"Ah, Clara. No offense, but I would have preferred Brigit."

"I'm sure you would. I saw you two canoodling on the beach," replied Clara with a laugh and raised eyebrows.

"Not for that," said Lucky, "my arm is broken in the same place as last time. I need Brigit to fix it before I can flash anywhere."

Although her ribs and head hurt from her recent scuffle with the guards, her light was as strong as ever, so the same rule about pain didn't hold true for her powers. She'd interrogated MacLir about how magic worked and where it came from, but maybe she should have asked Lucky.

Opening her mouth to ask her flood of questions, she was interrupted by Amy's overly loud, frantic sending. "Clara! Are you in range? Are you okay?"

"Quietly, Amy. I have a headache. I'm nearby, stashed in a closet with Lucky."

A long pause followed, and Clara assumed Amy was relaying the information to Brigit. Then, her sending much quieter, Amy explained Brigit's new plan. Clara, in turn, laid out the plan to Lucky, who eagerly agreed.

Opening her mind as if trying to hear Amy's sending from far away, Clara raised the light in her palm and waited. While Brigit and Amy were linking through their fertility magic, she could almost feel… something. When the link finished and Brigit's healing magic flowed through Amy, it filled Clara with soothing warmth, calming her headache to a more tolerable level. She didn't accept all the healing, instead quickly redirecting and gathering most of the power to the light in her palm. She waved the light over Lucky's arm so his injury passed through it several times. His face smoothed, and his arm looked stronger as repairs took hold.

The power slowly faded from Clara's hand, leaving only her fingers tingling. "That's all I have," she told Lucky. "Is your arm fixed?"

"Not completely, but well enough," he replied, stretching his arm out in front of him and flexing his fingers as he tested his range of motion. "Thanks, Clara. Thank the other girls, and let them know I'll be back as soon as I can find help."

With a slight pop, the god of travelers disappeared. She'd seen him do it dozens of times, but she'd never been so close to him when he did. The air around her sucked into the space he'd been occupying. Then, her light dimmed as she reached the edge of exhaustion. She let it go out, sent Lucky's message to Amy, then lay down on the ground to rest, using a bag of supplies as a pillow.

The darkness around her, the dull ache in her ribs brought back her headache, and her mind turned to past darker times. Her overtired, stressed brain held out memories for her inspection. She'd had pointless fights with her husband, said the wrong things at past jobs, and got upset at her children when she didn't need to. "Oh, yay. Past failures. That will help me sleep. Thanks for that," Clara mumbled to her mind. Her brain shrugged and offered yet another memory. The image of her recent failed attempt at being a wise leader of the group ended in what she realized was probably a cracked rib.

She could feel depression hovering, ready to swamp the logical side of her brain with only emotions. "No," she told the despair, "not right now." It lingered anyway, not descending but still threatening. She did her best to ignore it, desperately searching for something else to think about.

Entirely alone for the first time since she left her husband, Clara realized she'd been using Amy as a crutch. She'd ignored all the sadness she didn't want to face and pretended everything was fine. Pretending she could be her old self without ever processing the incidents that led her to this state of mind. All alone in the dark, she could find no distractions, and all the feelings overwhelmed her.

Tamlin

Tamlin shifted in the uncomfortable chair and crossed his legs. He glared at the sea god in the cage, the cause of all their troubles. The creature had played along, accommodating and chatty with the guards, but he was not fooling Tamlin. The pure evil in him would show at some point.

"So, you are the High King here?" the monster asked, his gentle boyish voice soothing and friendly. Tamlin braced for a trick but nodded. "Does that make you Cian's son? You don't look like him, but perhaps you take after your mother?"

A memory washed over him. He was plucked from the nursery at a young age, told he'd have a new father and brother, taken to the High King's house, and introduced to an already old Ian. Other than the new white jumpsuit they'd forced on him, it was nice for a time... before the lessons started. He'd had no idea how scary the outside world was. Filled with monsters. Like humans and the terrible sea god.

Tamlin had always been told the creature was not human, but MacLir looked so much like a man. It was not as he'd pictured the sea god. Ignoring the question about his background, he countered with one of his own. "Are you hiding your true form, sea creature?"

MacLir's eyes shone, and he smiled as he calmly said, "This is my true form. I don't have any other."

Scowling, Tamlin felt the man must be lying, for how else could the god he'd heard so much about come across as so kind and charming? Maybe his beautiful aqua eyes were a trap? Tamlin looked down, just in case. His duty was to make the monster release them from the Otherworld and one day lead his people to living aboveground.

Duty. He both loved and hated the word. He had promised his dying foster father he would carry on the cause. Carry on the duty to lead. What he'd been trained for his whole life. It was only after the man was dead and the plan initiated that Tamlin was told the actual plan. Ian would find the crow goddess, begin the revolt in the Ireland tunnels, then cast the spell that would kill all the humans. Including Ian himself.

Guilt flooded Tamlin all over again. He knew Ian carried no love for him after being passed over as Cian's heir, but Tamlin should have saved his foster brother. He could have sent the sea dragon with a message. He could have gone himself... but no. It was not time yet for him to leave. That was all in the plan, every step outlined. Ian had been deemed a necessary sacrifice but ultimately failed in his mission.

Tamlin would succeed with the backup plan now that his brother had failed with his father's preferred plan. Somehow they would get out from under the sea god's reign. His rule over their people would soon come to an end.

"It's because of you we can't live under the sun anymore. Why have you held us in the dark for so long?" Although Tamlin wanted to jump straight to the question of how to break free, he craved the answer to this burning question first.

"I only offered sanctuary to the Tua De. I have no hold over where they live."

"Lies," hissed Tamlin. His father repeatedly told him that everything was the sea god's fault. "We can't leave this place, and it's your fault!" However, a nagging thought tried to break through his tirade. Hadn't Ian left? The sea dragon was always coming and going. He couldn't seem to connect those events with this conversation, though.

MacLir frowned for the first time. "Why can't you leave?"

The sea god's concern seemed genuine, which only confused Tamlin further, but he knew the ready answer to that question. "The High Leaders say that the mortals outside are dangerous."

"You say you have humans here. Do they seem dangerous?"

Tamlin mentally reviewed the captives in his home. Beaten down and sad while cleaning, cooking, and tending the nursery. "These mortals are different."

"How?"

"Because the High Leaders say so."

"Right."

Ignoring the mild contempt in the MacLir's one-word rebuke, Tamlin thought of all the humans he'd met in his lifetime. Most were upset about their new life, but some embraced their roles. He'd become friends with the woman who made desserts. In her past life, she'd never had time to bake, but now she had endless time to create whatever culinary masterpieces popped into her head. He would miss her tarts when she was dead.

"Unfortunately, we must kill all the mortals and half-mortals."

The sea god was unsurprised at hearing the plan, the monster. He probably decimated entire cultures for fun. But, for a sentence that brought such sadness to Tamlin, all MacLir said was, "Why?"

"Our generals say they all must die, so we can be safe."

"Do you think those leaders might be wrong?"

"No," said his mouth. Yet, the thought of silk flowed in his mind, soft and beautiful. Who would make silk and custard tarts if all the humans were gone? In fact, humans did most of the work for the Tua De. Who would have stepped into those support roles if Ian had been successful? It alarmed him that he didn't know the answer and was missing information on that part of the plan.

Ian didn't die from the sacrifice magic, but he could have. His father and generals had made that choice and not bothered to tell Tamlin, their new High King after Cian passed on. He wondered what else those old men planned for him that he didn't know about.

Or, maybe it was simply that he'd never been told that part of the plan. After one more moment of worry, he turned his back on MacLir. He decided his father's generals were probably not deliberately keeping anything secret from him. He was High King, so all he had to do was ask for details. Because they were all working together for the sole purpose of making a better life for their people.

CHAPTER 10

Hazel

After a refreshing weekend of quiet with Emma, the two arrived at the appointed time in their common room. Hazel was getting used to the new jumpsuits. She hardly missed her dresses anymore. Mostly.

Crowding into the room with her team and feeling ready to get back to fighting practice, she was puzzled to see the whole room's color was changed. When they'd been given blue armbands as a promotion, their room's decorations were changed from brown to blue. Today no hint of blue was left, and everything was orange.

An excited chatter ran through the team as people whispered about what the new color could mean. No one had ever seen orange armbands before. Some older leaders marched through the door, marked by their green armbands, followed by the few teens in blue armbands that were the public face of the movement. The whole group arranged themselves along one wall, and Hazel's team turned to face them, lined up in three rows of five like they had been taught to do in the presence of the leaders.

"Today, you get to prove your loyalty," announced one leader. "You will be accepting an oath. I will say the oath, and you will agree by saying yes, and my men will watch to make sure you do so. Understand?"

The team nodded, and leaders moved to arrange themselves on each side of the rows.

"Let it begin," said the man and then clapped, a sound overly loud in the small space. "Each of you promise to never cease avenging the wrongs done to your clans at the hands of the humans."

"Yes," said the team. Enthusiastically, if a little off sync.

"You promise to obey the laws of The Pure."

"Yes," said the team. Their voices matched better this time, and Hazel felt a sprinkling of magic shiver through the room.

"You promise to give all your time and talents to The Pure and agree to accept any task you are given. This oath will bind you, your children, and their children."

"Yes," said the team in perfect unison. Good thing she didn't plan to have any children. She would have hated it if her mother had also taken an oath that bound her.

"You promise to cut your own throat if you disobey any duty set for you by your leaders."

"Yes," said the team, the perfect unison they found last time carrying them through this repetition. It wasn't until after she'd said yes to the others that she grasped what was promised. The man said she'd kill herself for disobeying? Had she heard wrong? She wondered if she could get a written copy of the oath and highly doubted it.

"It is done," said the officiator, clapping his hands again. Hazel's breath was pulled from her lungs, and blue lighting-like energy crackled on her skin. A burning smell filled the air. Terror pounded in her chest. Unlike the others she'd participated in since joining, this oath had been magically binding. Not only another fun part of the group's training. What had she promised?

Taking shallow breaths, she frantically tried to remember. It had not seemed too bad when he said something about avenging, which she'd already planned. Something about obeying, which she was already doing. A penalty for disobeying didn't matter because she wouldn't bother. Something about her children, which she didn't plan to have. Actually, she didn't see an immediate problem with anything she'd agreed to. Only proven her loyalty, and that was all an oath was supposed to do anyway, right?

The energetic warrior-girl from the first rallies stepped up to rousing applause and whistles. The fact that the rest of her team wasn't worried reassured her. Emma held her hand while the girl began her speech.

"Congratulations on your dedication to the cause! Imagine with me the future that awaits us. We've been fighting for the chance of a normal life. Above ground in a regular house. A home with our loved ones in the community of Tuatha Dé Danann. A neighborhood full of trust in ourselves and each other."

Hazel's hand was squeezed tight, and she saw Emma, overwhelmed with excitement and fighting back the tears of giddy bliss. The picture painted did sound fantastic. A regular life with the people she loved. It was worth any oath she had to take.

"Dream with me! Of a world where you can pursue your goals. A place where your personal choices are respected. No more worrying about where to live, where your next meal will come from, or what new laws might be forced on us from the High Court."

The cave Hazel was raised in came to mind. The permanently muddy floors, both in their cave and the clan's common room. The one meal a day they could count on made through the daily labor of her parents. Of course, this was all the High Court's fault for not standing up to the sea god.

"Join me proudly in wearing these new orange armbands to show your loyalty to the new world we're building together. It's time for a final battle with the humans. Because, as they've shown us, peace with humans is impossible. Let's change our future together!"

As the new armbands were passed out, Emma, standing tall and with happy tears still in her eyes, snapped her new armband on Hazel. Hazel took hers and did the same for Emma. Somehow the trading of armbands, their new status symbols, made the moment like a silently promised oath between them. Emotion swelled in Hazel's chest, and she let her happy tears fall.

They would change their future, no matter what it took.

Piper

Cycling between frantic and furious was getting Piper nowhere. Everyone had been gone for hours, and the only thing keeping her from following them was Clara's last faint sending that said to stay put.

What if she could have helped, though? Fia was acting so oddly, but Piper was sure Fia liked her. Maybe she could have talked through the dragon's problems. Now that she hadn't followed, she didn't know where to begin looking. If she left to search, she could leave the group stranded when they returned. The circular logic went around her head repeatedly until she had a headache.

Emily was down for a nap, thank goodness. Now all she could do was scan the horizon and worry. She saw the ripples before she saw the dragon. Fia's black eyes broke the surface near the ship, with ears laid back and scales clacking wildly.

"Fia! Where is everyone? What happened?"

The dragon refused to move closer but pushed words into Piper's mind, something it had never done before. "Awful," it whispered, "something awful. So sorry. Had no choice." Hearing the words this way, Piper could sense the deep sadness and horror the dragon felt through the mental connection.

Dread rolled through Piper's chest. What had Fia done? Hoping her new family was at least alive, she pushed as much kindness and understanding into the front of her mind as possible. She sent back, "I understand you had no choice, but tell me where MacLir is."

Reassured, Fia moved closer and, in a whimpering childish voice, said aloud, "They forced me. They make me do things. They created me. So long ago."

"I understand, Fia, but… is MacLir alive?"

"Yes, yes. Alive," said Fia happily, tail flicking in the shallow water. Then, adding, "For now."

Piper clutched the ship's edge, the inset rough emeralds and sapphires biting into her palms. Then, keeping her tone as steady and calm as possible, she said, "Start over. Tell me everything."

"I was made by an island nation. Modified from my ancestors, turned into something new before hatching. The seas there, they are full of my kind in various forms."

Holding in a sigh, Piper ground her teeth and began rocking. She wanted to hear everything about what happened to MacLir and the others but refrained from interrupting Fia's story, and the dragon continued.

"Like you, I get future images. Mine is limited to what will help a project be a success. I see the useful tool to create success. Tool could be spoken words, a found object, or… sometimes… a person, like you."

Piper considered how they first met when Fia had pretended to be stuck in a net, then insisted Piper go with

Lucky. She wondered what vision of Fia's had sparked that encounter. Also, had she already been the successful tool, or did she still have an important role to play in a successful project?

"In the Island Nation, some want war with other islands. War-wanters were cast out. Told to take ships and two dragons and leave. They bring me with them here. Other dragon gone, now I'm alone, but I have you as a friend?"

"Yes, Fia, I'm your friend," confirmed Piper, but her mind was racing. She remembered MacLir telling her the Tuatha Dé Danann legend had them arriving in ships from the sky. Apparently, this was only a small group of them, and there were more somewhere?

"All war-wanters travelers gone too. No one left, just their children. Lots of children and more children. The children control me now like the first outcasts did. I obeyed my first masters but didn't want to obey children of children. Not a puppet. Not."

"I know how that feels," said Piper. She was glad the days of people telling her what to do were over. Especially her domineering father. Making her own choices was wonderful. She had no idea her friend was being controlled for others' use. That sounded even worse than her earlier life.

"I do their visions, and I tell them truth as they order me," said Fia sadly, shaking their scaly head. When their scales stopped clacking together, the sea dragon smugly added, "I do my own visions, though. My own project is to get away from them. Delivering friends to bad Tua De was the tool. They also give orders to deliver. I must obey, but also want to obey this time. My project vision is same as their orders."

Fia's broken speech was even worse than usual while agitated, and Piper had difficulty following the story. It sounded like Fia willingly gave them MacLir to help with the dragon's long-term escape plan. Piper set that aside to deal with later. For now, she still didn't have full details about where her family was located.

"I save you, though! You are not required for my plan, and you would be hurt bad with their plan. I lie some, tell them you not on the island. After I move you off the island." Fia's huffed chuckle was endearing, and Piper smiled in return. "Caused me pain, though. Always hurts to disobey. Hurts and hurts, then fades. I'm okay now. And you okay now too. All good."

"Not all good, Fia. I need MacLir back. And the others."

Fia considered. "No. Gone. All gone in the underwater tunnels. I can't follow, and you can't go. They would kill you. Sorry, sorry. They gone."

Now that Piper knew MacLir was in danger, she wanted to run to his rescue. Logically she knew the dragon was right. She couldn't go. Who would tend Emily if she rushed blindly in? If Fia would even lead her there. "Well, we must do something!"

"We will," said a voice from the cabin doorway.

Fia and Piper jumped and swung around to see the voice's owner. Lucky stood tall, back in his usual dark, fitted clothes. Gone were his vacation shorts, replaced with everything from his ironed vest to his long sweeping coat. His sword, The Answerer, was strapped to his back.

"How long have you been standing there?" Piper managed to say as she tried to calm her heart, drumming with joy that at least Lucky had managed to escape. It gave her hope.

"I heard much of the conversation. Fia, I recognize that you didn't have much choice in your part of today's trickery. I accept that your betrayal was forced and appreciate that at great pain to yourself, you saved Piper."

The relationship between these two had never been good. Piper watched them uneasily come to their new understanding of each other. Fia's ears were pinned back again, but slowly their great head moved closer and touched Lucky's outstretched hand.

"Yes, yes. Am sorry," whispered Fia.

"I know," replied Lucky. "Now, let's go rescue our friends."

CHAPTER 11

Tamlin

Tamlin acknowledged the remaining evening workers as he passed the processing areas on his daily rounds. They only had a few more humans to assign, then everyone could rest for the evening. Not that anyone here could see the sun marking night and day, but they had stolen clocks to keep them on track.

It frustrated Tamlin that everything was stolen, right down to people. Even himself. He didn't know who his real parents were because he'd been adopted by the High King so young. Most days, he tried not to worry, but talking to the sea god today had cracked his carefully built wall of reasoning. That and the silk dress. He didn't want the pastry chef to die either.

He'd finally found a general to ask who would take over the captive's duties after all the humans were gone. However, he only received reassurances that, "everything is being taken care of, and as High King, you don't need to worry about such things."

Arriving at the kitchen, he was greeted by the pastry chef, who smirked as she asked, "Can't stay away from my new tarts, can you?"

"I can't withstand the pull of any of your tarts, new or otherwise." Tamlin grinned as he swiped one off the trays near her.

She chuckled but didn't stop him. His eyes lingered on the orange armband she wore. He could not imagine who would do all the menial chores without humans. He'd once heard a disturbing story about the Ireland clans. They'd outlawed capturing humans because it brought too much attention to themselves, so now their half-magics and poor had to do all the work. When he heard it, he'd shrugged it off as a rumor, but now he wondered.

"You seem distracted today," his friend pointed out, handing him a plate full of tarts.

He nodded his thanks, accepting the plate and wishing he could save at least this one human. Not only because of her excellent skills but also her friendship. Tamlin was raised with no friends and wasn't allowed to have long conversations with anyone or even know their names. These stolen moments with the chef or his second-in-command got him through the days, but if he was in charge, couldn't he change things?

He smiled and raised the plate in appreciation before leaving the kitchen. Heading to his room for the night, he passed through the throne room and around the cage that held the sea god. The creature was relaxed and confident, almost as if MacLir was allowing himself to stay captive. Tamlin doubted he could be so calm in the same situation.

Too many things were not adding up. Usually, in the evening, he'd enjoy his tarts with his nightly devotional study of the words his father wrote while king. The past of the Tua De in Ireland and even further back. Before they'd arrived in the human realm. His father also wrote out many various schemes for the future, plans with backup plans that spread and crossed like lines on a map.

He had copies of all the books his father wrote over the many long centuries in their underwater home. However, Tamlin usually ignored the future plan books. They were written by a man who was near the end of death and frustrated about his life. Rambling and full of plots, they were confusing at best. Tamlin had not read the books all the way through. Preferring to read about the past and leaving the planning to the men his father picked. Although now he didn't know which plan the generals were following.

Maybe if he could study the books, he'd figure out which and perhaps locate a better plan for his people. Setting his plate down next to a comfy armchair, he turned to his bookshelf to locate the planning books. As he found each one, he added it to the pile on the table next to the plate. Four in total. All were written in the old Tua De language and transcribed by an elderly brown armband that his father had pressed into service.

He had a long night ahead of him since he was not planning to sleep until he found a way to save his tart maker. With his treat and reading material ready, it was his favorite part of the evening. He opened the massive trunk at the foot of his bed and stroked the soft fabrics inside. A white silk shirt and sturdy brown pants that had come with a red brocade vest were one of his favorite outfits, even though he knew that was no longer the fashion of humans. The new captives they had caught recently had even more refined clothes. Then he remembered the latest dresses.

Opening the bag with the two new pieces of his collection, he laid them on his bed. Which to pick tonight? The yellow chiffon called out to him, but he decided to savor the anticipation and leave it for another night. Then, carefully tucking the beautiful fluffy dress into the chest, he turned back to consider the green garment. He admitted to himself it was almost as wonderful.

Removing the shapeless scratchy jumpsuit was a relief every night. Sliding out of it as quickly as possible, he tossed it out of sight behind him, satisfied when he heard it thump against the wall. It was probably in a messy wrinkled heap on the floor where it belonged. It didn't deserve any better treatment.

Reaching for the green dress, a thrill ran through his chest. The silky fabric slid over him, the softness of it giving him giddy shivers where it touched his skin. It was simple in design but elegant in its simplicity. The fabric swept up and over only one shoulder, leaving his other shoulder bare, to flow straight down and sweep the floor. The height fit him perfectly, and when he zipped up the side of the dress realized the waist was an excellent fit as well.

He wished he had a mirror but knew the dress was as perfect on him as he'd hoped. Sitting in the armchair and crossing his legs, the thigh-high side split in the dress laid his knees bare. It made him admire the clever clothing designer, and he almost switched his plans to pour over his other collection of books. The ones with all the bright photos of humans in their world, in so many different styles of clothing.

No. Instead, he would find a way to save them. He sighed as he read over the book's first few pages on top of the stack. It was the most recent one written. Barely coherent ramblings of a man he had once admired, but Tamlin was unsurprised he found nothing useful. Then, shuffling through the stack, he found the first book of plans. It was still mainly rambling, but it contained some good points.

Tamlin knew the generals were itching to get back to Ireland and use the power to finish the spell Ian had failed to complete, but he was convinced there was another way. About halfway through the book, Cian finally stopped waxing long about killing the humans who had tricked his people and seemed to also realize what Tamlin was recently worried about. Through the texts, it looked like he'd spent a little time wondering if a small group of humans could be subdued and kept as captives to do the cooking and cleaning. Finally, the book outlined the plan, and the next entry was a small note about their success in carrying the plan out. Instead of killing the humans in the captured ships to steal their goods, the past clans also began keeping the humans. To control them by beating them until they agreed to work for the Tua De.

Tamlin knew it worked. He'd attended the public beatings and occasional killings that kept all the other humans in line. It was easy enough to kill and replace one troublesome human with another. If his father had realized this, it meant his people must have been doing upkeep before the humans. He could not imagine switching to a system like that. It would feel like failing as a leader to see his people so degraded.

He studied the pages with his father's idea of quelling the humans. They would, of course, have to kill most of them, but the important part was that not all of them would go. It was a good plan. He read the pages several times, memorizing all the essential bits and adding his own flair to the new course of action he would talk the generals into.

Finally satisfied with his discovery, as Tamlin bit into his last mini tart, his door burst open unceremoniously.

"High King, the women in the nursery, are starting a revolt, and…" his second in command trailed off as he finally took in Tamlin's evening activities and attire.

Tamlin hastily dropped the remainder of the tart on the plate. It landed with a thunk and clatter, loud in the stillness as both men seemed to stop breathing. Then, jolting up from the cozy leather armchair, his father's book fell to the floor, and the skirt flowed around his bare ankles.

His second in command, Sam, didn't move. Instead, he seemed frozen in place, his eyes serious. "You look lovely."

The naked emotion in Sam's voice caused Tamlin's cheeks to go warm, spreading to the tips of his ears. He wondered if his cheeks were a rosy pink like the photos in the books. He wondered if Sam would like to see his books about clothes. Then he remembered what the man had said, something about a revolt.

Standing straighter, Tamlin asked, "Is everyone okay?"

"For now, but we must get everyone out."

"Out? What do you mean?"

Sam gave him a shy smile, and his eyes crinkled, "I'll step out while you prepare yourself to lead. See you in the tunnels."

Then the boy was gone, quietly shutting the door behind him. Tamlin been seen in human clothes, but Sam didn't seem to mind. In fact, he liked it. If clothes for the High Leaders were not wrong, maybe a fondness for the human tarts was also fine? Even a fondness for the tart maker? Perhaps more than a fondness for his second in command. If all of his favorite things were actually okay, what if other teachings of his father were wrong?

Clara

The door opening woke Clara from her nap. She didn't remember falling asleep, but instead of feeling rested, she became disoriented. Her fuzzy brain tried desperately to process where she was, what she was lying on, and why the light was flooding the doorway of the newly opened door. A man filled the entrance, and she heard Lucky's voice. "It's time to break out of here."

Pulling Clara to her feet, Lucky half dragged her out of the dark storeroom and partway down the hall before she halted. "I'm not a child. I can walk on my own." Lucky glanced over at her when the sudden lack of motion jerked him backward. "What's going on? Have you brought help?"

Odin, the elderly god of war, popped into existence next to Lucky. His gray beard, gray clothes, and eye patch gave him away based on the description Piper had told her, even though Clara had never met him herself. His grayish driftwood staff pounded the ground in irritation a couple times as he growled, "What's the holdup? Fia's got water pouring in, and you're standing in the hallway yapping."

Lucky looked between them and took off again down the hallways calling behind him, "Follow me!"

Clara hastily trailed him but glanced back and saw Odin pop out again. She put on a burst of speed and caught up with Lucky, demanding, "What in the world is going on?"

"Odin is mobilizing the captives, Sam is gathering his people, and Fia is breaking the glass domes. We need the nursery women ready at the last dome they break to ensure the children get out safely."

"How do you want us to prepare them? I don't know what to say."

"Can you do a reading on yourself?"

Clara knew Amy and Piper could read themselves and wondered why she'd never tried. Her steps slowed as her power took over her mind, and she saw a vision of herself speaking. She didn't need to say the words out loud. They gave her enough courage to follow Lucky around the corner and begin mental planning to organize the women to escape their underwater prison.

"When you get the women ready, pray to Odin, and he'll lead you to the right exit," said Lucky, and then he disappeared too.

CHAPTER 12

Clara

Clara stood outside the nursery door, taking a moment to wonder where the guards were. Then burst into the nursery, calling for Amy. Her sister popped her head out of the nearest doorway, the sitting room Clara had been dragged from.

"You're back!" Amy stepped forward for a hug, then hesitated. Clara was grateful for her sister's moderation and her understanding that sometimes Clara was not in the right frame of mind for a hug. At this moment, though, all of Clara's sadness from the year caught up with all her fears. After being dragged out by the guards and left in the dark, with and without Lucky. She stepped forward and pulled Amy into a tight hug, fighting back the tears and trying to regain the resolve and urgency she'd had a moment before.

She opened her eyes to see Brigit smiling at them and stepped away from Amy. Then, it was time for action. "Gather everyone here. Everyone."

Brigit started down the hallway as Katherine appeared from the room. She had heard Clara's words and looked as if she could not decide whether to chase after Brigit or argue with Clara. Arguing won. "I give the orders around here," she declared.

"It's time to leave. You could help."

"Really," said Kathrine sarcastically. "What would you have me do?"

"Gather the women."

"Why?"

"So I can talk to them. It's time to escape."

"No," said Kathrine smugly, a smile on her face.

Clara could not identify the look on Katherine's face. She was usually better than when she was younger, but she had much practice over her lifetime. Still, Kathrine's face was confusing her. "No? But don't you want to see the sky?"

"This is home. We have everything we need here. I don't need to see the sky or anything else you want to show me!"

Clara was shocked. Was it possible other people felt as Kathrine did? Deciding to do a makeshift survey, even as she worried about the time, she turned to a woman in her early thirties who was pregnant. "Hi. My name is Clara. Given a chance, would you escape?"

"Of course, I would leave. Wouldn't everyone?" she rubbed her belly and talked wistfully down to it. "I was captured seven years ago, and even though I've found love here, I would leave in a heartbeat."

As Kathrine rushed away to stop Brigit, Amy helped with a quick poll of the women in the sitting room. Anyone who'd been captured wanted out. Anyone born here had no concept of escape or where they would go if they left the caves. It was time for a speech, but Clara wondered how best to gather everyone.

Doing another quick reading on herself helped. Then, hurrying to the room across the hall, she found the kids she'd seen in her vision. These were the oldest children in the nursery, nearly five years old. Clara explained to as many children as would listen that it was a holiday and they needed to gather everyone by the front door.

"We aren't allowed to go past that door," said one little girl.

"Today is special. Today you get to leave the nursery." The children became more interested. "I need you to spread out to every room in the nursery, and every person you see, tell them to go to the front door. Can you do that?" The kids nodded eagerly. "Then go!"

Forty pairs of toddler's feet stomped past Clara as women gathered by the door. Even when Kathrine tried to stop it, everyone came. Human curiosity is nearly as powerful as human belief.

When everyone was gathered, Clara began her speech, wanting to address them before they lost interest. "Today is the day we leave the caves to—"

"Don't listen to that liar!" Kathrine pushed her way through the crowd of people filling the wide hallway. "Go back to your rooms, right—"

"Let's hear her out!" shouted Amy, cutting her off.

Other people from the crowd added, "Yeah!", "Let's hear it!" and "Speak!"

Clara lost no time in complying with the encouragement. "The men are fighting each other! I have three friends out there leading the fight, and before it even finishes, the tunnels will be flooded with seawater. You will return to the surface where people are meant to live! Gather what items you need and gather the children! We are leaving in two minutes!"

She had their attention, but now what? Everything she'd said was confident and true, but the women were visibly wavering, looking between her, an outsider, and Kathrine, who was preparing to take over. What did these women need to hear? Clara wondered what she could say to make them believe in her and follow her to a better life? She'd never tried to see what to say for multiple people at once, much less a crowd, but she prayed now to whatever gave her magic, human belief or the universe, and saw a vision.

"An amazing world exists that some of you remember and some can only imagine. We must be strong to reach it. Hardships make us strong when we get through them! When we challenge ourselves, we become stronger! We are all strong women! And the time has come to prove it to ourselves!" Everyone was smiling at their friends and nodding. "So prepare yourselves. My friend is destroying this place as we speak, so if you want to get out safely, it's best if we go together and stay in a group. I'm leaving in two minutes, so anyone who wants to live needs to gather their things and follow me."

The women rushed away, and Clara leaned against a wall, lightheaded in exhilaration laced with dizziness, and prayed to Odin to let him know they were ready.

Kathrine's purple face showed her anger as much as her quivering voice when she hissed, "How dare you! How dare you gather everyone without my consent to give them false hope! There is no way out of here! I'm close to a High Green, and he told me—well, what he told me is none of your business! But we can't get out!"

Odin popped into being next to Clara, causing more than a few people to jump and others to back away. Although Odin looked like a bum in his wrinkled gray clothes and flyaway gray hair, he had a commanding presence.

"We need to hurry," rumbled Odin. "Lucky helped MacLir first escape, and now Lucky is over-enthusiastically helping Fia with the dome breaking. Half of these caverns will shortly be underwater. Well before we planned for it, I need to go."

"Who will lead us?"

"Here's the map you need to follow, the path to the dome of attracting station number two. MacLir will meet you there."

"How will he know when we are there?" Clara asked as she examined the map. When Odin didn't reply, she looked up, but he was already gone.

Tamlin

When Tamlin left his room, he was unsurprised to see MacLir's cage empty. However, he was startled by the ankle-deep water that he sloshed though to get to the far door. It occurred to him that they were perhaps naive in trying to trap a sea god in underwater caves.

Dashing down the hallway to the communications room, he was shocked to see Sam tinkering with the door controls. As he watched, his second-in-command typed in the codes for all doors to open. Even the cages and water containment systems. In response, more water surged down the hallways, soaking Tamlin's shins through his jumpsuit.

"You can't open the water containment doors during flooding!"

Sam smashed the machine's control panel, then turned to meet Tamlin's eyes. Shoulders back and in his leadership stance. Sam was rebelling. Destroying everything his father worked to build. "You weren't supposed to see this. I told you to head to the nursery. They are evacuating early there, and you'd be safe."

"I should have you killed, whipped at least…" whispered Tamlin.

"You wouldn't," replied Sam. "You are a kind man. A good leader."

"That's right, I am the leader. I am the High King. I must uphold the rules." Pain cracked his voice. If he'd caught anyone else destroying the door system, the person would be severely punished, probably sentenced to death by the generals. Sam was the one person that could not be punished. At least, not by Tamlin.

"You don't have to be in charge. The texts are all made up, written by your father to bend minds to his will. As he was always so good at doing. He's gone now, and we're waking up. We don't have to follow anyone." Sam ripped the blue armband from his jumpsuit to prove his point and let it drop to the floor.

"No," said Tamlin, beginning to tremble. The cold seawater swirling around his knees was not the cause of the coldness flowing through him.

Sam stepped into the next doorway but reached out a hand. "Shake off your brainwashing. Come with me."

"Stop," said Tamlin. He didn't want his friend to get hurt, which would undoubtedly happen when the generals caught up with him. If everyone was not drowned by the leak in the tunnels.

Sam's hand dropped, but instead of leaving, he waded through the water, stopping less than a foot from Tamlin. "At least help me get everyone out of here, and then I'll find you on the outside. We could... be together."

Tamlin had seen a book recently where a whole page was taken up by the photograph of a city at night. With little twinkly lights lining the road. Two people walking away through the lights had their hands intertwined. He reached for his second's hand and tangled their fingers. "I have responsibilities. I must continue my father's plans for the good of all the clans."

His second leaned forward until their foreheads touched. "Oh, Tam," Sam whispered, a twinge of regret in his tone.

A tingling ran through Tamlin, both at the touch of Sam's head and hearing his name. No one had called him his real name since it was announced he'd be the new high king. If Sam knew it, he'd snuck through the records to find it. A smile touched the corner of Tamlin's mouth as he stared into Sam's matching green eyes.

"Hopefully, I'll see you again someday," Sam said, pressing his lips gently to Tamlin's.

He realized he might love Sam if this was what love felt like. However, the moment passed too quickly. Before his brain could catch up, Sam was halfway down the hallway, shouting orders to some men running in the wrong direction.

Tamlin picked up Sam's armband, still floating in the water, and tucked the soaked scrap of fabric into his pocket. Sam was both right and misguided. It's what Tamlin had been working on all night. It was a new plan based on his father's old plans to bring his people back to glory, but with new twists added.

He could not follow Sam right now. Instead, he needed to lead his people to safety and victory. The Great Leaving was happening sooner than planned, but now that he had a new strategy, the timing was not as important. They could leave today, and everything would be fine.

He sloshed his way to the communication panel and got a message to their Ireland crew. Let them know the base was in chaos and that they evacuate the high court to the prearranged location much earlier than arranged.

The Great Leaving should have been a celebration of abandoning the sea caves forever. It would have started with a party. There would have been lots of tarts. If only Sam had confided in him, he could have explained more of the plan, especially Tamlin's new part about saving some humans. Now everything was rushed, and he didn't know if anyone would survive.

He'd felt torn after his talk with the sea god, putting doubts in his mind. It was worse when one of the generals he liked refused to give him information. For one moment, he wondered if maybe Sam had it right, but no.

He was done with everyone telling him to want to do and what to think. Not only was Sam doing the wrong thing by siding with the enemy, even if Tamlin wanted to join him, he could not. The wheels were already in motion. The generals would wipe out all the humans unless he stayed High King and put his new plan in place. Tamlin was more sure than ever that he was the right king for the job.

"We are changing our future," he whispered as he turned back down the hall to rescue his favorite vest and father's books from the flooding.

CHAPTER 13

Clara

The women dithered about what to take with them, and her two-minute deadline passed. "Everyone ready to go should already be standing outside," said Clara firmly.

Amy obediently stepped out into the hallway and shrieked. The wordless cry of alarm got Clara's feet moving toward her sister in time to see the ten-foot wall of water barreling toward them. Amy held out her hands, her head tilted away from the water, eyes shut tight.

"I will not die of drowning," announced Amy, the power of belief causing a worry line across her forehead. The water halted, rising up against an invisible barrier. "Even so, tell those slowpokes to hurry."

"NOW. We're leaving now," called Clara. "The water is here!"

All the women gasped as they saw the water swirling at the end of the hall, splashing against a glass wall that didn't exist.

"I have to lead them," said Clara. "Can you hold that back while running?"

Relief flooded through Clara at Amy's strained, "Yes."

Brigit added, "I'll stay behind and watch over her."

Taking the lead, Clara began to run the route she had memorized from the map. Left, right, right, through a double door, left, left, left. Sometimes she checked for her sister's dark hair at the back of the group and saw the water following them. Crashing in foamy waves near the ceiling, the water bounced off the walls and the barrier of Amy's belief in magic.

She turned a corner and bumped into a man in a white jumpsuit. Panicked that they might be caught between their captors and the wall of water, she glanced up to see his armband rank. She was starting to work out who was important based on the color band they wore. He didn't have one. Meeting his eyes as the group bumped into her from behind, she saw it was Sam.

"This way," he said, grabbing her hand to keep her from being trampled and dragging her through the space to another set of open double doors up some stairs.

From the doors, the tunnel sloped sharply upward, so Clara left the leading to Sam, and she stayed in the entry to make sure all the women got through. Brigit nodded to her as she darted elegantly past the doorway.

Her sister was last out of the hallway, the water only a few feet behind her. She held it in the hallway as she ran up the stairs, grabbing Clara's hand and pulling her up the sloping tunnel. This was the third person today to touch her without asking, but the one she minded least.

They both looked back to see the water flow out of the hall to fill the large space, lapping at the bottom stair and quickly rising to the top stair as more water flooded in. They ran, hurriedly escaping the torrent. They dashed up the rough-cut tunnel into an unbroken glass dome much larger than the one they'd been captured in.

It was full of people. Humans and Tua De gathered in groups, but she didn't see the High King anywhere in the crowd.

The giant dome shifted, and she felt the same sensation as going many flights up in an elevator. After rocking to a halt, glass cracked low on the left. The crack spread outward, spiderweb fine.

"Everyone will drown!" someone screamed.

Clara looked back the way they'd come. Water was lapping up the tunnel, not quickly, but visible enough that it was a threat, so they could not retreat.

The glass shattered. Shards sprayed inward, but the water held steady outside the dome. Clara looked at Amy, a question in her eyes. Was Amy holding back the whole ocean? Amy shook her head with a shrug.

MacLir popped his head around the jagged glass, water dripping in his eyes, and bellowed, "MOVE! NOW!"

Clara led, modeling the behavior she wanted from the crowd. Sprinting to the hole and she dived into the water being held back by MacLir. She was pushed from behind, and in moments lifted to the surface by something large. A gray dolphin gave her a deliberate toothy grin before diving back under.

While treading water, she watched more and more heads pop up around her. The sun shone down, blinding her after the dimness in the underwater caves. Amy swam over to her, sending, "Did you feel that?"

Clara hadn't felt anything. She examined herself and the water around her anxiously.

Amy bobbed nearby, flailing in the water. "We were just pushed from the Otherworld. We're all in the human realm. Look." Clara's mind rang with Amy's mental shout. Treading the deep water and trying to keep her mouth out of it as much as possible, Clara shaded her eyes and peered in the direction Amy pointed. Ships were heading towards them. Many boats of various sizes with a helicopter above them. All are marked as the US Coast Guard. It was a relief to know all these people would be out of the water soon, but it made her think. There hadn't seemed like enough people waiting in the dome, surely not everyone who lived in the caves.

Before the glass broke, she remembered that even though the vast dome was big enough to fit an aircraft and had been packed with humans and Tua De, she had not seen the distinctive High King. In fact, she hadn't seen many blue armbands in the crowd and almost no green armband wearers. So, in their escape, had they accidentally killed half their captors? While she didn't love how they'd been treated, she didn't think they all deserved to die.

Someone grabbed her from behind and pushed her under the water. She automatically gasped in shock, taking a breath and bracing to feel the water in her mouth, but only sucked in the air. The bubble around her head was appreciated. However, she would have to talk with people about grabbing her arm without her permission, even in urgent situations.

When Clara noticed the sea dragon in the water, the creature ducked and came up underneath her. She was forced to hold Fia's ears again or roll off into the water alone. MacLir was ahead in the sun dappled water, holding Amy with one hand and Brigit with the other.

Fish hurriedly darted out of the way. Even slow-moving sharks sped up to avoid Fia zooming past them. MacLir halted in the water when land loomed in front of them, but Fia didn't stop and tumbled Clara onto a sandy beach. MacLir and the others followed slower, the air bubbles surrounding their faces popping when they touched solid air.

Clara surveyed the small jungle island with a huge cave

opening, and sitting on either side of the cave were Lucky and Odin.

"They're gone," said Lucky, pointing out to sea. A three-story yacht was visible in the distance. "I've flashed too much. I'm too exhausted to keep following them."

"It's okay," said MacLir, "let them go. We can guess where they are headed."

Clara was relieved to know the other half of the underwater residents had not died, but she had a twinge of worry about what havoc they might cause if they joined with the Ireland troublemakers.

"I'll get Piper," said Fia, disappearing into the water before anyone could reply.

Amy fell into the sand, and Brigit headed up the beach to sit close to Lucky, but adrenaline was still pumping in Clara, and she wondered what could be in the cave.

"I'm going exploring. Come with me?" she said to Amy.

"Pass," said Amy, wiggling deeper in the sand.

"I'll go! I'm always up for some exploring." MacLir smiled and walked with Clara into the cave.

The sun was beginning to set, shining light on the island's west side. The east-facing cave was deep within the shadows. Clara held out her hand, turning on her magic light, and holding it aloft to see into the gloom.

"Hmmm..." said MacLir beside her. He twirled his finger in a circular motion, and globes glowed in the ceiling, lighting up a large room with support beams. MacLir and Clara both gasped. Piled and stacked against the walls, beams, and even scattered on the floor was more treasure than Clara could have ever dreamed of.

Steps went up to a doorway on the far side of the room, presumably into the flooded caves of the underwater Tua De. She realized the treasures must be what was taken from the planes and boats over the years, from people like the poor women in the nursery. "This is the stolen wealth of living people. We can return it to them."

"Not all the owners are still alive," said MacLir, picking up an antique in perfect condition.

"Still," Clara said, "these items will go a long way to giving all those people a good start, especially those who don't know how the world works."

The deeper into the cave they went, the more lights MacLir flicked on above them. Clara had never been to the faerie mounds but thought these indirect lights might be similar to stories Amy had told her. When they reached the metal ship in the back corner, Clara dropped to the sand in shock.

A silver and copper saucer sat in front of them. The structure was twice as tall as a human and four times as long. Bright silver with a coppery sheen, it was like nothing she'd ever seen. "It's a…" Clara hesitated, not wanting to say what she was thinking out loud, but the words aliens darted around in her brain.

MacLir's hushed voice near her ear said, "Legends say the Tuatha Dé Danann came to conquer Ireland… from the north. Which could also be translated to mean… they came from the sky."

"The sky," Clara repeated softly. "Is this really… a spaceship? What do we do now?"

MacLir laughed. "Do? What do you mean?"

"Aliens exist! Shouldn't we tell someone?"

"Who would you tell? And if you did, who would believe you? Besides, humans make metal ships too, so who is to say the ship came from other stars?"

With a more critical eye, Clara examined the seams and bolts of the machine. In fact, the more she explored it up close, the more it reminded her of a welded train. "Do the Tua De make machines?"

MacLir shrugged. "It's possible they might have, long

ago, even if they don't now. I can't recall their arrival, but the legends say the ships that came were surrounded by dark clouds or perhaps smoke. Although, that would have been well before humans created any kind of machine."

Clara ran her hand over the smooth metal ship one last time. A magical group of conquers from the sky? The intriguing image danced in her mind, both puzzling and terrifying.

CHAPTER 14

Piper

Regrouping at Amy's home was the easiest thing to do, but the tiny two-bedroom house was bursting at the seams. It was filled with seven adults, a baby, and three dogs. However, instead of being frustrated, the group found comfort in being safe together. Robin let them know his most recent information-gathering visit had been perilous enough that he'd decided to stay away, maybe permanently. So, Lucky and Brigit could not return to the tunnels. The situation had become even more unstable in the group's short absence, although it seemed as if most Tua De were uniting under one thought pattern. Anger at MacLir.

Piper was glad the big new house was nearly finished. Before they'd left for the island vacation, she'd visited the building site with MacLir and could see her vision taking shape. It would be another month before they could move in, and she wondered if staying in Amy's house the whole time would be possible. It was reassuring to see everyone in one place and know they were all okay, even if most everyone was sleeping on the floor.

Currently, the whole group was crowded around the television. Lucky and Brigit were close together on one side of the couch, Clara on the other. Amy reclined in an armchair with Robin leaning against her legs on the floor. MacLir and Piper sat as close as possible, propped against a wall, Emily sleeping on a blanket next to them.

An in-the-field newswoman stood with her back to the water, the sunset lighting the sky with vibrant hues of golden yellows, oranges, and pinks behind her. Her brownish hair blew in a sea breeze, and as she spoke, the camera panned out to show bedraggled people wrapped in blankets walking down the ramp of a ship. The image reminded Piper of how her new family had looked that morning. Straggling into the house dripping wet, covered in sand, and wrapped in blankets. When Fia told her they were ready for rescue, Piper pushed the ship faster than ever to pick them up at the island before anything worse happened.

The newsperson's overenthusiastic chatter broke through Piper's drowsy thoughts. "I'm coming to you live from Florida, where the cruise ship survivors are de-boarding the Coast Guard's boats behind us. The Coast Guard, responding to an anonymous tip, located an unconfirmed number of people. After the break, we'll come back with an interview to tell us more." Rescue footage followed of people in the water supported by dolphins. Then, the screen shifted to bright moving colors advertising a new drink.

Clara muted the noisy commercials, and no one spoke in the silence. It had been an exhausting day, and Piper began to drift to sleep, but her eyes popped open when the sound came back on, and she saw the same newsperson speaking with a man in a blue uniform. He said in a formal and stern voice, "In talking to the people recovered, we have learned they were not ever on a cruise ship but are members of a lost civilization. Some say they were captured, others call themselves the Tuatha Dé Danann, and they are numbered in the hundreds. So we're calling every organization we can to feed and clothe these people while it's decided where they will go."

The overenthusiastic news lady pulled the mic back and said, "There you have it! Exciting times! We'll continue to bring you updates as we get them. Back to you in the studio."

Piper's eyes drifted shut again as the in-studio news anchors chatted about what this could mean. When she woke from her doze, the news was still on, but the room was filled with early morning light. She was lying on the floor, blankets wrapped around her. She could feel MacLir behind her and tilted her head to see Emily with Vixen curled protectively around her.

Clara was lying on the couch with a blanket and pillow, watching the barely audible news. When she noticed Piper's movement, she said, "Oh, sorry, did I wake you?"

"Maybe, but it's okay," said Piper. At her words, MacLir stirred, and Vixen's ears twitched. Piper decided staying at Amy's house for the month was not going to work. She couldn't sleep on the floor that long, but maybe they could pay extra men to get the big house done faster? It was comforting to know that everyone she cared about was under one roof, but she knew their current arrangement was temporary and everyone would want their own spaces sooner than later.

When Piper sat up and stretched, Vixen lifted her head and yawned. A big canine yawn that showcased all her teeth and long curled tongue.

"Thanks for taking care of Emily," sent Piper to the dog.

"Someone had to," replied Vixen testily in her British accent. "The other dogs here were about to trample her. Great louts."

Piper scooted over and scratched Vixen behind the ears and under her chin and promised to build the portable crib next time. Then, picking up Emily, she settled into the arm-chair to feed the infant and asked Clara to turn up the television.

A morning talk show was on, just coming back from break. "So, what do you think about the astounding news of a new civilization, Joe?" A woman host asked her male counterpart.

Joe sat back in his chair and crossed his legs. "They claim they are responsible for the Bermuda Triangle myths and intrigue, but how would a lost race know anything about modern urban legend? The answer to that is as odd as their abrupt appearance. Half of the recovered people identify themselves as Tua De, short for Tuatha Dé Danann. The other half say they were taken prisoner and used as free labor by the Tua De! They claim their efforts are what created the enigma of the Bermuda Triangle! To add further mystery to the tales, some of these people went missing only weeks ago, while others say they were born as far back as the early 1800s! We'll learn more when we bring a couple survivors onto the show tomorrow morning. Ashley, have you heard about the committee formed to help the hundreds of displaced people?"

Ashley turned from Joe to the camera, saying, "I think it's wonderful! A committee was put together and authorized by the government to sort the Tua De community, issue or reissue IDs, and put families back together. So many young children were separated from their parents that DNA testing would be done on everyone to reunite them. The committee is asking for donations. Clothes of all sizes, canned food, and monetary donations are welcome and can be sent or dropped off at any of the addresses on your screen."

Clara glanced at a wall clock. "If we go after breakfast, we could be back by the evening news. We are still donating all that treasure from the cave, right?"

"Yep!" said Piper.

Clara yawned. "How are we going to give it to them? We can't unload it from the ship in plain view!"

Both of them jumped when MacLir answered from the floor, "I have a plan." They'd forgotten anyone else was in the room, asleep or not. MacLir's mischievous grin showed that he knew that, and Piper grinned back at him, shaking her head.

The loading of Wave Sweeper with a cave-sized amount of treasure had exhausted everyone, despite all participating, even pulling out the rarely used ramp instead of the rope ladder.

After Lucky had scouted out where donations were being accepted, MacLir parked Wave Sweeper on the Otherworld realm side of the parking lot. He outlined his plan, and everyone got to it.

They started by laying out several tarps on the ground and putting the ship's ramp in place. Then, the women dropped lightweight things over the railing to Robin and MacLir. At the same time, Lucky carried the heavier and delicate items down the ramp. When the deck was finally cleared, everyone dressed in their best clothes. As representatives of the triple goddess, Brigit, Clara, Piper, and Amy gathered in their dresses. At the same time, Lucky donned a fresh shirt and vest. Even MacLir put on what Piper called her favorite pants, the brown pair with laces up the sides instead of his usual swim trunks.

Settling Emily in a crib with Vixen to watch over her, everyone left the ship in the Otherworld to drag the tarps into the human world. Then, creating a linked hand chain, with one hand in the link and one hand on a tarp, they materialized inside the donation center near its big double doors. The volunteers were speechless, taking in all the priceless antiques and treasures. Their eyes were huge, and one finally said vaguely, "Do you need a donation receipt for tax purposes?"

Lucky grinned, and MacLir shook his head. "Please sell these items on behalf of the rescued, then give each adult and child an even portion."

The group of gods and goddesses turned and walked out of the warehouse. Then, while still in sight of volunteers, MacLir pulled them all into the Otherworld.

"MacLir," growled Lucky, "stop showing off."

MacLir only laughed. "So they saw us appear and disappear. What can it hurt?" Piper hoped he was right.

Clara

"What are we going to do!" wailed Amy, putting her face in her hands.

Robin rubbed her back as Lucky said, "I knew it wasn't a good idea to disappear in sight of all those people."

MacLir looked down at the infant sleeping in his arms. "It's my fault. I should have known there would be security cameras."

"It's no one's fault. Our disappearance only adds a thrill to the news," said Clara. "A large and strange donation would have landed in the evening broadcasts anyway."

"They don't have any of our names, only a video clip. So, what's the problem?' asked Piper.

"True. You're right," agreed Clara, wondering if they were overreacting. "Let's go to bed early tonight, and I'm sure things will look clearer in the morning." Everyone nodded and drifted away from the television.

"Sage wisdom," mumbled Amy as she was led to their room by Robin. It made Clara grin at her sister, who gave her a half smile. Everyone else returned to the ship's comfort, leaving Clara and the television alone.

Despite being the calm voice of reason, Clara was worried. Flipping through all the American and local channels, their faces were featured on every program. Either it was scheduled news or breaking news, but there they were. Clara thought she looked good in her deep blue goddess dress. The metallic sparkle on all their dresses attractively caught the sunlight through the open doors behind them. Then, poof, they turned and faded away.

It was human, after all, being scared of what was different or unknown. It's why the magical community had been guarding against discovery for centuries. Avoiding notice and, therefore, persecution. So, while Amy was loudly worried about the harassment it might bring them, Piper also had a point. The media didn't have names, only a short video.

Clara flipped to a new channel, dazed when she saw a close-up of herself. The military facility they had visited for donation dropoff obviously had excellent cameras, which had easily zoomed in on the video to clearly show their faces. "This woman has been identified by the survivors as Clara. An American claiming she's an Irish goddess of wisdom, the same as her American sister, Amy."

Worry shifting from a case of nerves to full-blown buzzing anxiety, Clara fell back into the deep couch with a groan. She vaguely remembered introducing them to the women in the nursery. One of them appeared next on the screen, pointing to a photo she was being shown, and said, "Oh, yes, that's Clara. She gave us a stirring speech that gave me the courage to leave. She was right, and I'm so glad we followed her."

Clara tried to feel joy at saving the woman's life but struggled instead with dread as each group member was named by different survivors who remembered them. Only MacLir remained unknown. Still, they only had first names. Clara had been a stay-at-home mother, Amy was still young, Piper had lived a sheltered life, and the rest were Gods or Tua De. The few people who could fully identify them were family members and unlikely to call the news to offer more information. Even if they did, none of their families knew where they lived. Clara turned off the news and yawned. No use getting worked up worrying about potential futures, she told herself. It was more important to focus on the present.

CHAPTER 15

Tamlin

The dimly lit hallway closed around Tamlin, and he tried not to feel claustrophobic. These dark rock walls with water dripping down them were dank compared to his home's dry, lighter, colored rock. Those wide tunnels had smooth floors with plentiful bright lights. He slipped into another patch of mud and cursed under his breath, grabbing the wall for support. He didn't fall, but the water on the cave wall soaked the sleeve of his white jumpsuit. No wonder the Irish clans were desperate to get above ground. He had lived underwater his whole life and never felt such pervading dampness.

The underground house he lived in now was okay. A guest bedroom in one of the High Court's homes was nicer than anything he'd ever seen in real life. The man's family and the entire High Court had been welcoming, but cloyingly. Tamlin had lived here for weeks, and today was his first outing alone, having slipped away while everyone else was finally distracted.

He'd asked directions to the kitchen some time ago but had not found a quiet moment to attempt the trip alone. Missing his friendly chats with the pastry chef, he was hoping the informality of the kitchen would present the opportunity of making a friend here. Not that he could only make friends with chefs, but it was all he could think of to ease the empty feeling of missing his favorite chef and his second in command.

The kitchens were everything the tunnels were not. Huge and dry, with good lighting and a calming mood. He'd timed his visit well, as only a few workers remained after dinner service. It was the best time of day in his kitchen at home to beg for a bedtime treat, and he hoped the same proved accurate here.

He'd done a few speeches already, and even if his face was not recognized, his embroidered armband got people's attention. Tamlin was approached by a heavyset woman with her red hair in a bun. "Hello, my name is Ginger. I'm the head chef here. Can I help you find a snack?" He liked her instantly. She was not bowing like most of the people he'd met. She was respectful, but in a way that made him think this was how she talked to everyone.

"I was hoping for… well… a mini tart? And…" he trailed off, not wanting to admit he was lonely but also desperately wanting to get to know the head chef. Or anyone who would treat him as a person instead of a position.

"Hmmm, we don't usually make mini tarts. However, when you arrived, I was planning to sit down with tea and cake. How about you join me?"

Tamlin breathed a sigh of relief as she led him through an archway to a cozy stone fireplace in front of two chairs. Pans hung along one wall above stacked cans of human food. Lights from above created a glow in the room, soft rather than dim. The floor was hard-packed dirt, yet everything looked clean, with a pleasant aroma of good food.

Eating the piece of thick cake from a china plate with a tiny fork, Tamlin felt his shoulders relax for the first time since he arrived. He stared into the fire, watching the flame flicker and shift. With a start, he realized he was not good company, but when glancing at Ginger, he saw she was also lost in thought. She caught him looking and smiled, her friendly eyes crinkling.

"The cake is excellent," he told her. He knew how much his friend liked compliments on her work, especially when they were true.

"Many thanks. You know, I've heard tell you are Cian's son, but you don't look a bit like him."

"He adopted me when I was young. Did you know him?" He tensed, waiting to hear what she would say. Besides his father's generals, no one seemed to have anything good to say about Cian. Tamlin had arrived expecting to hear wondrous tales of his father's glorious godly triumphs. Instead, he learned Cian wasn't even a god, just a regular trodden-down Tua De like he'd seen all over the mound during his tours and speeches. He was a womanizer, a cult leader, and, depending on who was talking, a criminal.

"Oh, sure. I knew the rogue." Clearly choosing her words carefully, she explained, "He won us many battles, but eventually, we lost the war to rule Ireland. He never took it well."

Based on the handful of stories Tamlin had pulled out of people, all of his father's lessons on austerity seemed like rubbish now. Blasphemy, his mind interjected, but against who? His father? Everything was so pointless. He'd been excited about the Great Leaving in the hope that he'd get to pick his own clothing in Ireland. Finally. Yet, he was always in the same canvas jumpsuit because of his father's teachings. They had made it across the water and infected all the clans with Cian's wild ideas.

Tamlin didn't want to think like this. Lost in the flicker of the flames again, he tried to grasp his belief in his father. His faith. It flooded into him, like putting his feet in a comfortable pair of shoes. Of course, these people would not appreciate all his father had done. They didn't see the underwater world he'd built for his clan, much better than what he'd left behind here. It was built on rules, and if it seemed inflexible, it was only to continue making the underwater tunnels into the best possible place to live.

His father had done well with what they had, but it was only meant to be temporary until the right time for his plans to unfold. Cian had put his faith in the seer's prophecies, Fia's obedience, his general's cleverness, and Tamlin to lead. So, he would do his part for the plan and more.

Although, everyone here was wearing such interesting clothes, and it was a misery to not even try on a scarf.

He wondered again if he should be trying to carry a conversation. But the armchair was comfortable, and the tea was warm and soothing. Trying to think of a safer topic than his father, he found himself admiring the soft-looking knitted stripy socks in teal and emerald the head chef had on. He'd never bothered trying on socks with his nighttime outfits and wondered how that would change what his shoes felt like. "I love your socks."

"Thanks, I made them myself," said Ginger, pulling up the hem of her dress to show them off better. "I could make you some in your favorite colors if ya like."

Tamlin smiled in return, saying, "Yes, I'd love that."

Hazel

Hazel stood in the crowd with her team of fifteen, their orange armbands marking them as part of the rebellion. She tried to ignore the collar of her brown jumpsuit, scratching her neck to instead focus on Emma's warm hand in hers. Everyone was facing the stage, waiting to hear the new High King speak, murmuring with excitement as the mic was prepared. Rows of his attendants and guards lined the area.

She had seen him around the tunnels but had not heard any of his speeches. From others who had been invited to them, it was said he outlined the whole plan, so she was interested in what he had to say. Trying to hold together belief in her new leaders and their new government was a constant stress because things she'd heard were not adding up.

Finally appearing on stage, the new High King stepped softly across the platform to the mic, the spotlight following him, glinting off the gloss of his wavy hair. His slim body was swimming in the shapeless white jumpsuit, but it didn't detract from the sparkle in his friendly leaf-green eyes.

Approaching the stand with the mic, he waved at the crowd saying, "Welcome, my friends! I am the High King of the Underwater Kingdom, created by Cian. Now, it's time for a final battle with the humans."

The audience roared and cheered with approval. Hazel and Emma join in, adding their voices to the hundreds crowded into the largest cave meeting room.

"Before we get started, let me introduce my staff. The green armbands behind me are Cian's generals, the blue armbands behind them are their second-in-commands, and the brown armbands surrounding us are soldiers ready for war."

The crowd cheered again, but Hazel didn't join in as loudly. Where were the orange armbands? She'd been told orange was a step up from the blue they had initially been given. Frustration bloomed in her chest. The speech was supposed to help her understand more about The Voiceless Pure, not create new questions.

"Because of MacLir, we can't live under the sun anymore."

Hazel didn't cheer at all this time, thinking so hard it was bringing on a headache. She'd been listening to Emma's rants about the laws and had not heard any reasoning for the anger against MacLir. The new High King didn't provide any proof either. Instead, he repeated the same tired lines she'd heard from the green armband leaders for months.

"Peace with humans is impossible, and they must pay for the treachery of their ancestors." Because Hazel was not screaming her throat raw with the others around her, she noticed how the High King's shoulders had a slight droop. How his feet shuffled. The words were correct, but he didn't seem to believe it.

"And we'll be even stronger when humans are under our control or dead," said the king, choking on the last word. He began to cough, and his personal servant rushed from the side of the stage with a cup of water. The human servant was wearing a brown jumpsuit and an orange armband.

Her mind struggled against what it meant for her future as the High King's feet shifted back and forth at her eye level. Hazel saw he was wearing brightly colored socks. Red and yellow knitted stripes stood out against his white jumpsuit and white shoes.

Somehow, this flash of color was the last straw. It broke her doubts out of the mental cage she'd been stuffing them into. It was all wrong. Everything was wrong. Even the High King must know it. She didn't know how, but his uncomfortable stance said what his words didn't. Hazel had been tricked. She knew it now. Slowly over time, but still.

She'd helped to stir up the clans against a god she knew was not to blame. She couldn't pinpoint exactly how, but she had gone from making a simple protest sign to standing in a one-piece jumpsuit, ready to fight humans. Of course, she didn't want to hurt humans or anyone.

The High King was finally outlining the plan, something about bombs and governments. She wanted to listen, but her thoughts reeled out of control. Anxiety stole her breath. She'd made oaths. Binding promises. She would not be allowed to back out now.

Hazel peered into the shadows of the stage wing and saw several people with orange armbands. Some were clearly human. One had the facial features of a half-magic. Her stomach dropped. She remembered, again, her grandmama's story, something about a Firbolg ancestor, but had never bothered to learn more. Her team was not going to live like gods. They were marked as servants to the pure-blood Tuatha Dé Danann.

She tried to point out the orange armbands to Emma, but her friend shushed her and pointed at the High King.

"For cities with the highest population, we'll need to do careful localized spells to destroy those with human blood that the bombs don't take care of. Then, we can round up remaining humans and combine them with half-magics for the workforce."

The crowd cheered again, but now she understood the triumphant restoration of their lands on the surface would not be for her benefit. It was not a return to the magical days of heroes but a way to enslave her if she even lived through the killing spells with her partial human blood. She examined the faces of her team and decided they had either not fully realized what he was saying or didn't care. Maybe they knew they were half-magics and had already understood what would happen?

Tears streamed down Hazel's face as she pulled away from Emma, who clung to her hand, asking, "What's wrong?"

Hazel shook her head, a tightness in her throat keeping her from speaking. She tugged so hard her fingers ached, and Emma released her with a hurt frown, then turned back to cheer the High King. Hazel ran.

Pushing her way through the crowd, she kept moving. Down hallways, cutting through great rooms, she blindly walked into a northern transport tunnel and found herself near home. When she heard her mother's voice around a bend, she ducked into the other fork of the tunnel. She'd instinctively headed home but was not ready to face her mother yet.

Hazel watched her parents enter the transport tunnel, south to the kitchens, dressed for work. That meant her grandmama would be alone in their cave, and maybe she could get some answers. She expected the elderly woman to either gladly greet her or give her a lecture. Instead, her grandmama nodded and said hello as if her sudden visit was any other typical day. Hazel wondered for the first time how old her grandmama was and if the woman was going a little senile.

Sitting on her old hard bed, she said, "Grandmama, did anyone come asking about our heritage recently?"

"Oh, yes. Some nice young men in white jumpsuits wanted to hear all my stories." Hazel's heart sank at the news. They must have heard something they didn't like, and that's why she ended up in a brown jumpsuit, even before being given an orange armband.

"Of course, it's hard to tell who is old and young these days," her grandmama continued. "Everyone is eating that magic pig meat. It's unnatural to have eternal youth. Vile. Against the laws of nature. You won't see me supping at that table."

Hazel was shocked to realize that she had never seen her grandmama at the feast. "You've never mentioned that before," she accused.

"Ah well, your mother forbade such talk in the cave, and I agreed to her wishes while you were young. She's the family's leader, taking care of you and me as best she can."

Hazel's mind, whirling to keep up from too many revelations at once, wrestled with this new perspective of her mother. As an average person struggling with worries—instead of a tyrant whose only purpose was to harass her child. Not sure what to do with this new information, she shoved it into a corner of her mind for review later. Right now, Hazel had important things to sort out.

Like how was she going to get out of the magic oaths she'd taken and didn't even fully remember the words. "I don't know what to do, grandmama," she whispered. "I feel so lost."

"Patience, young one," said her grandmama with a yawn. Then, laying back in her bed with her eyes shut, she added, "Everything happens at its own pace. Sometimes, the best course of action is to wait and watch."

Hazel decided this was good advice. The longer she stayed away from her team, the more she felt a magical tug to return to them. It was starting to prickle her skin and sting her lungs. With nothing to help break the spell at the moment, she'd have to wait and watch for a way to escape.

CHAPTER 16

Clara

"The builder did an amazing job," sent Piper to Amy and Clara as they passed another elegant twisting staircase.

"The builder is balding," sent Amy amused, as they were led through an elaborate arch into a kitchen.

"Rude. It's not like he can help it," replied Clara. "And Piper, you could say your praise out loud. I'm sure he'd love to hear he did a good job."

Piper smiled at Clara, sending, "You could say it. I can't interrupt their tour. But honestly, though, I really do like the houses." The group followed the builder and designer out the other side of the kitchen into the next of the four interconnected homes, awed by the size.

"How does it manage to look modern and Victorian without clashing those different decorating styles?" sent Amy, examining the intricate wooden paneling along the ceiling.

"Maybe paint colors?" asked Piper.

"Maybe you should ask the designer," pointed out Clara, but she knew she wasn't bold enough to move to the front and ask either. Her hesitation must have flowed through with her comment because Piper and Amy playfully grinned at her. She rolled her eyes at them in Lucky's favored expression, which Brigit caught sight of, recognized, and chuckled even though she could not hear their conversation.

The women continued to trail the men, eagerly following their tour guides through the new empty houses. Clara had never been in a building with so much light. Since the three-story houses were a perimeter to contain the courtyard, the four thin houses lined the outside of the property. So, all the rooms had windows on both sides letting in abundant light, one side facing the countryside or ocean view, the other side showing the interior courtyard garden and Wave Sweeper's parking spot.

"It took much longer to finish than I wanted it to," complained Piper, the sending filled with impatience.

"At least it's done now, and we're moving in this week." Clara tried to fill the message with soothing calm. A calm she sometimes even felt these days, with hope for a peaceful future. The house would be a haven from everything they were all running from. Living permanently in the human realm, away from the discontented faeries, frustrating human families, or the media. "Fortunately, a house out in the country is well away from anyone who might recognize us from the news stories."

The news continued sensationalizing all the human interest stories as the month had passed. Lost and found children, romances before and after the rescue, emotional after-effects of being captured, happy reunions, and families finding new homes. Clara shook her head at the ongoing coverage but admitted she could not help being fascinated by the stories either. None of the people received privacy until they permanently settled somewhere. Integrated into a county of their choosing.

"At least they stopped showing our pictures on the news, mostly," sent Amy, with an audible sigh that made Robin briefly turn his head toward her. She waved his attention away.

"Did you hear the new theory that some think it was a trick to get media attention and more donations?" asked Piper, eyebrows raised and a smile playing on her lips.

"I did hear about that," put in Clara. "It's a relief that the incident is only occasionally referred to these days. I think we've probably hit an end to the whole mess. And speaking of ends, I think we reached the end of our tour."

"...last payment due," the builder was saying.

MacLir shrugge. "I don't have it handy today. Can you come by for it later?"

"I'll be on a new job across the country, but you can drop it by my office anytime you are ready."

MacLir shook hands with the man and saw them out the door. Then, turning back to them with a broad grin, he announced, "We have a home."

When the cheering subsided, Clara watched the other couples hug and kiss. She had a brief flash of nostalgia, remembering celebrating moving into a new house with her husband, almost wishing he was there, and yet... no. It was calmer this way without entanglements.

She noticed Piper's unfocused eyes trained on her, then they shifted to sadness. "Stop trying to find a man in my future," she told her friend. "I don't want one."

"That's good because your future still doesn't have one." Piper's sending was mostly grumpy, but it didn't completely cover up the sorrow the Goddess of Love also felt over Clara's mateless future. Clara mentally shrugged, but outwardly smiled to reassure Piper. She had no intention of starting up another romance because, after eventually healing, she was fully aware she didn't have the mental strength to start over again.

Piper

Smooth door, bright cold window, rough wallpaper, soft curtains, and back to smooth door. Piper circled the room again, her fingers trailing along the textures of the four walls. As she considered how to decorate the nursery, Emily sat on a blanket in the room's center, watching her circle.

This was everything she hadn't known she wanted growing up. Hadn't dared to dream. A loving partner, an adorable child, a permanent home, and a loyal family. The house was still unfamiliar, but she was looking forward to a lifetime— or multiple lifetimes—getting used to it, making it hers, and raising Emily here. She was finally truly hopeful about the future.

On another circuit of the room, she noticed Wave Sweeper land. Picking up Emily, she pounded down the stairs to the kitchen and arrived at the same time as MacLir, who had a worried frown. "I think I shocked the building office receptionist."

"What happened?"

"I went in, gave her my name and address, she looked up our account, and I left while she counted the money. I parked Wave Sweeper in the Otherworld, and even around the corner, well out of view, so no one would see me disappear—"

"Learned your lesson, did you?" interrupted Piper, with a belly laugh at MacLir's embarrassment.

"Yes, well, all my preparations were for nothing. She came running around the corner shouting about a receipt, just in time to see me vanish."

"So? What's the problem?"

"I'm not sure… it's just that… she didn't look shocked or surprised, more like she was plotting."

Piper laughed. She could rarely understand people's expressions, except MacLir's after living with him so long, but she would not be able to recognize plotting. After all, what would that even look like? She posed the question to MacLir, but he merely shrugged and reached for Emily, dismissing both the encounter and his unease. Piper wished she could let go of anxiety that quickly.

"There you are! Where have you been? Have you seen the news?" Amy came running in and stopped babbling only because she was out of breath.

Piper motioned they would follow and found themselves in Amy's front room for a repeated breaking report on an all-day news channel. "…video was released to the press, and it is our top story this afternoon. So let's show it again."

Amy's pacing, seen from the corner of her eye, distracted Piper, but she tried to pay attention to the television screen where a woman in an expensive sitting room was stroking a tiny dog. "I want a baby," the woman announced. "I know a girl who said a magical being named Amy caused her to become pregnant. I'm offering a million-dollar reward to anyone who can tell me the accurate whereabouts of this being."

A number to call flashed on the screen, and the woman faded as the news anchor returned. "This video was sent to many news stations last night and has been broadcasted worldwide today. Most agree that Amy is the same person named as one of the groups in the video of strange disappearing benefactors last month." During his speech, the video played again, showing closeups of all their faces. "Again, if you have information about Amy, call the number on your screen. Also happening today was the—"

Clara shut the TV off and said, "Amy, you gave someone your name?"

All eyes turned to Amy, still pacing with her face twisted in mental anguish. "She was chatty. I'm chatty, so we talked. She was so nice. I'm sure she didn't mean it would get out of hand if she told someone about me. What now? What happens next?"

"Nothing," Lucky declared. "Nothing, like last month when we were in the news. Any neighbors who recognized us respected our privacy and will do so again. No one else who knows us also knows where we live. We can keep an eye on the news, but it will die. Same as before."

Piper's daydreams drifted back to the rescue and the media after. So that was not a one-time thing like she hoped it would be. This new occurrence proved it. Now the world knew about them, would they ever be left alone?

MacLir cleared his throat theatrically, saying, "Actually, someone saw me vanish today."

"So?" asked Lucky, his arms crossed and his eyes narrowed.

"Well, it was about two minutes after I'd given the lady my address, and if she'd already seen this news story… well…"

Lucky opened his mouth to say more, but a loud banging at the front door took them all by surprise. They edged closer to the door, and Lucky cracked it open.

Piper moved to the window and saw a crowd of reporters and news cameras. From all the uproar on the front steps, she only heard a few clear sentences from several people, but they made her heart sink.

"Is this the home of Amy?"

"Does Amy live at this residence?"

"Is she the Amy who helped rescue the Tua De?"

"Do the other gods live here too?"

Lucky tried to slam the door shut, but one person got a microphone and foot in the door first. Lucky's back tensed and his eyes glowed green. He glared through the crack in the door. "Move back, now." The man moved so fast he tripped, falling against several others crowding in.

"Piper, get away from the window," said Lucky, his eyes still glowing, but he'd put no coercion toward her, only seeming worried about her safety. Now she was concerned too. She could hear more vehicle doors shutting and a roar from above that sounded like a helicopter.

"The whole house is windows," she muttered, trying to remain calm. He'd already turned away, striding back to turn on the television.

"Wave Sweeper!" MacLir dumped Emily into Piper's arms and raced for the nearest door. She returned to the television in time to see the helicopter footage, marked "live," of MacLir sprinting through the newly planted vegetable garden and disappearing simultaneously with his ship. The news people gasped.

The video shifted with a tag that said "earlier" to show Lucky's growl at the media. His eyes glowed green as he demanded, "Move back, now."

The anchor came on. "If you are just joining us, this video was taken only a moment ago at a large estate on the southern coast of Ireland. Responding to the request from billionaire Carol Alexander, a tip led to the previously unknown residence of Ireland's most influential legends. Saint Brigit, Manannán MacLir and Lugh Lamfada, and the modern goddesses rescued hundreds of people from the Bermuda Triangle only a month ago. The tip and information were provided by a temporary worker who would prefer to remain unnamed but is now waiting for confirmation of her information to get the million-dollar reward. We're going now to Stacy, on the scene."

A reporter stood outside Amy's side of the house where all the reporters had gathered after the door-opening incident. The mass of people behind her seethed with frenetic energy. Each was doing their own coverage, taking photos inside any uncovered windows, and making a mess of the new lawn. Numerous reporters and camera crew lingered in the background, ready for something interesting to happen.

"I'm outside the mansion waiting to speak with someone from the house behind me. We are trying to discover the names of the mansion's occupants. To confirm if it belongs to Amy, the Goddess of Creativity, recognized by both the rescued Bermuda Triangle victims and the anonymous tip today. Communications from our air team lead us to believe we have the correct house. Strange activity in the house's courtyard was taken moments ago." At her words, a popout with the video of MacLir and Wave Sweeper disappearing came on again.

"Couldn't you have done that from the house?" Clara asked MacLir as he returned.

"No, too far. In hindsight, I realize I could have used the Otherworld to get closer, but… I saw my ship on the TV and just…" he sighed.

"This is outrageous! I'm so angry!" Amy began to pace again. "Who does this woman think she is to use the media to harass us! She has no idea who we are! I'd surely feel it if she wanted a baby that badly!" Robin folded her in his arms. Despite the cacophony outside, in the cocoon of the nearly silent house, everyone could hear her muffled voice add, "I'm angry that I brought it on myself and all of you."

"What do we do now?"

"Nothing, same as last time," said Clara, repeating Lucky's words from earlier. "We eat dinner and go to bed. They aren't going to break in, right? So, eventually, they'll go away."

"Humans are curious, and I don't think they'll leave for a long time. We have to put a stop to this. Now," said MacLir.

"I agree," said Lucky.

"But how?" Amy asked. "It's too large to ignore."

Piper waved her arm for attention. She didn't often talk in a group, even this one, so when she did, people listened. "I have an idea. What if… we accept the media?" Amy's eyes narrowed, so she held up her palms defensively. "Let me explain. People are staking out the house because we're a mystery. If we come out and say, 'Yes, we're here, then won't they mostly go away?"

"It won't stop the madness on the news," said Clara.

"But we'll be able to control it better," pointed out Lucky. "If we acknowledge they are there, we can order them to go away."

"We can ask them to go away," corrected Brigit, tugging playfully at Lucky's ear.

Lucky growled. "Fine, ask. Back in the day, we had respect from the people. So they might do as we ask if we tell them who we are."

"If it doesn't work, we'll have to abandon the house," warned MacLir. "We could all live on the ship until we worked out something else."

Piper's stomach sank. She didn't want to backtrack when she'd finally achieved the only goal she'd had since running away. A permanent home. "We must at least try to save the house. What if we not only tell the media to leave but actually answer the call for help from that lady? Wouldn't that calm things down?"

"Maybe, but if that doesn't work, we leave," said MacLir.

Amy pushed herself to her feet. "Okay. I'm convinced. Let's go." Before anyone could stop her, she marched through the entryway and threw her front door open to the cameras.

CHAPTER 17

Tamlin

Wiggling his toes allowed Tamlin to feel the fluffy yarn Ginger had used to create his newest pair of socks. The texture was a distraction, so he tried again to focus on the generals as they droned on.

He'd heard this bit already, and he'd have to patiently explain his new plan to them. Again. These people needed to remember that the most important part of any plan was putting the right people in place and that he had been chosen. Tamlin was High King, right? He was at the head of the table. So, he should be in charge.

Losing patience, he interrupted the old man to his right. "Yes, thank you for once again explaining the details of the old plan," he said, emphasizing the world old. "However, as I've explained several times over the last week, I've made adjustments that must be considered when deploying bombs and troops."

One of the Ireland clan generals toward the far end of the table muttered something, and the woman across from him rolled her eyes in agreement. All Tamlin could make out were the words "mere boy," but it was enough. The two slumped forward, heads banging against the table as Tamlin roughly knocked them out. He could have done it more gently but had wanted to make a point, and now they would have headaches on waking.

Their friends cried out in alarm, apparently forgetting that the 'mere boy' had stronger power than most people in the room. Even if it was limited to temporarily shutting down brains into sleep. "I don't want either of those unbelievers at our next meeting," instructed Tamlin. "If anyone else feels the same way, you are not welcome. The door is right there if you wish to leave," he said, pointing to the only exit.

A murmur ran through the room, but Tamlin ignored it, pressing on despite the whispering. "I understand many of you are disappointed in the new plan. It's not as… flashy as previous options. However, you still get to use the bombs you gathered. And you still get to have a war with many humans, just not with all of them. I'm certain I've made myself clear today and in the past several days." He looked around, seeing stunned faces and others conversing in hushed tones. "The next person who talks over me like I'm not here, or tries to insert pieces of the previous plan, will find themselves sleeping in a way they won't wake from."

Silence now greeted him from the table. His elders, many of them older than even their faces showed, kept their eyes downcast. He suspected more than a few were glaring into their laps rather than showing actual submission, but it was enough.

"This is one of our last planning meetings, and I want to tie up loose ends before things are set in motion. Is there any new information I need to know?"

A woman raised her hand, standard Tua De in appearance with rich brown hair and green eyes. "We have located the home of the sea god, or rather, the humans have located him and his allies. They are all living together in a big house in Ireland."

Tamlin had been worried about the sea god messing up their plans, even though no one had seen the monster since the underground kingdom flooded. They could send the first bomb there if they knew where he was. "Good. That will make them easier to kill. Thank you for the information. Anyone else has anything they want to add? No? Then our meeting is concluded. Think about what I've said, and remember who is in charge of the next meeting."

He walked out of the room and down the hall, pausing when no one else emerged from the room as well. He shrugged and let out a small sigh. They probably wanted to sit and complain about him for a moment. Cian's generals had often done that, sometimes even before Tamlin could slip away. As his father always said, they didn't have to like him. They only needed to obey him.

Meandering down the various tunnels, he came to a fork. He could go to his guest bedroom or the kitchen. Choosing the kitchen, he kept walking while thinking. He had not told Ginger about his life or his plans. They chatted about types of yarn instead of how his army would conquer the whole earth. He wondered why. One tiny part of his brain offered that he was not actually satisfied by being in charge, but of course, that had to be wrong. Tamlin was a proud foster son of a great leader and would take over where his brother had misstepped.

The future was difficult to predict, and there had always been a chance his foster brother would fail in the spell to eliminate all the humans. Tamlin was glad Plan A was unsuccessful and that he'd had time to adjust Plan B. It would be enough to include preserving some of the humans using the combined assistance of every single follower. The bombs, originally only intended for the opposition of magical folk not killed in the spell, were now sent to all mortal governments of wealthy countries. That list also included their own High Court meeting room and, of course, the home of the troublesome god of the sea.

Clara

The high and mighty baby-hungry billionaire was only the first. After Amy's initial acknowledgment of their existence and explanation of their powers to the press, it opened the floodgates to humans asking for assistance.

Piper got letters from thousands of lonely people asking her to find them a mate. "I'm not a dating service!" she said when three hundred letters came in one day. Amy received letters from mothers wanting children, but she could do nothing without a link to their minds. Brigit's letters told sad stories of loved ones with incurable diseases, begging for miracles. Clara's letters outlined complicated stories from people interested in advice on what they should do. Some offered to pay for the goddesses' services. Others wanted both a miracle and some treasure too.

"The more people who believe in us, the stronger our magic is getting," Brigit pointed out after a week's worth of letters overflowed a trash bin. "What if we actually answer some of these?"

Sifting through the letters to find one they each wanted to try that wasn't too far away, the women all scheduled visits for the following day, but the men declined to participate.

Lucky shook his head at them while they prepared to leave, saying, "It's a fool's errand."

"We'll stay to guard the house," said Robin. MacLir quickly nodded his agreement, cuddling Emily tight as the goddesses departed.

The first couple they visited had been trying to have a baby for eight years. Amy left them with assurances that it would finally happen.

Next on their list was Brigit. Leaving Wave Sweeper in an empty parking lot, they found the address and crowded onto the front step.

A man answered the door, introduced himself and his family, then invited them to sit on the couch. When they were all seated, he said, "My daughter was recently diagnosed with cancer and given only a few months to live. She is only seventeen." He dropped into a chair, covering his face with his hands as silent sobs wracked his body.

Brigit sat cross-legged on the floor next to the daughter's armchair. "I've never tried to heal cancer before, so I make no promises." Brigit took the girl's hand and closed her eyes. The parents' optimistic expressions faded as thirty minutes rolled by. Clara tried not to imagine what it would be like to have been told one of her teens had something incurable. She hoped they were doing okay in college and decided to call them later.

Brigit was actively sweating and had a grayish tinge to her skin when she finally sighed. Shaking her head, she leaned against the couch edge for support.

"I found the dark places. I made some shrink, but I could not make any go away completely." She rubbed her forehead, and tears sprouted in her eyes. "I started out so hopeful…"

A vision of wisdom swept through Clara, and she per her hand on Brigit's shoulder, informing her, "Remember, hope itself can be powerful."

Brigit sniffled as she stopped crying and considered the piece of advice. Then, taking a deep breath to calm herself, she returned to the girl and held her motionless for another fifteen minutes. Clara became worried when Brigit swayed. Although her eyes were firmly shut, she still had her hand solidly on the girl.

When she fell boneless to the carpet, Clara mentally screamed, "LUCKY!" She could only cross her fingers that praying to him worked the same as it did for Odin.

A second later, he appeared with a sword in his hand, ready to strike out. He saw Brigit on the floor, seemingly unharmed but with exhaustion on her gray-toned face. Lucky lowered his weapon, shaking his head at her overextending herself, and handed the sword to Clara. The father opened the door for Lucky as he carried Brigit out, and Clara told the family, "We'll, um, be in touch."

Brigit was awake but still resting when they arrived at the following location. "I think it's in the apartment building," said Piper, landing the ship in a mostly empty parking lot.

Clara and Piper wandered down the long hall of doors with Piper muttering, "Twenty-one ten, twenty-one ten, twenty-one ten… ah ha! Twenty-one ten!" She knocked confidently on the door, and it was promptly opened.

The girl in the doorway seemed close in age to her own grown children. Wearing jeans, a solid-colored tee shirt, and a dark brown ponytail, she reminded Clara of a shorter version of Piper.

Clara glanced over at Piper, but her eyes were unfocused, so she stepped forward with one hand on her chest as she introduced them. "Hello, my name is Clara, and this is Piper."

"Wow, you actually came! I'm a little embarrassed to have asked, but I hoped—"

"Oh!" said Piper. "We have to go! Now!" Running down the hallway, she turned back and waved for them to follow. The girl bolted after her, and Clara internally chuckled at the younger women. Shutting the girl's front door, she followed at a slower pace.

Making her way up Wave Sweeper's ladder, Piper called over her shoulder, "Hurry, Clara! Or we'll be too late!"

As soon as she was on board, Wave Sweeper shot up and away. Then, landed outside a large building on the other side of town. Piper continued to lead the way as they burst through the doors into a huge indoor mall with a staircase curving around a beautiful water fountain. The fountain splashed high then into a wide round wishing pool glinting with coins.

Piper looked around, then marched toward the pool. "Just be yourself… and sorry for this part," she told the girl.

"Sorry for what—"

Piper pushed the girl toward the pool while simultaneously sticking her foot out to trip her. As the girl fell, Piper seemingly accidentally collided into a boy with copper skin. When he turned to see who bumped him, he saw the girl falling into the fountain. With excellent reflexes, he reached out and managed to grab her. First, rescuing her from the water, then setting her on her feet.

The young man moved around to face her, his arm never leaving her shoulders. "Are you always so klutzy?"

The girl blushed. "No."

"Well then, my name is James."

"Hi. My name is Mindy. Thanks… for the rescue."

"I was on my way to the food court for lunch. Are you hungry?"

"Um… yes?"

"Would you like to join me?"

"Yeah," Mindy said, nodding in agreement.

As they walked away, she looked back and smiled appreciatively at Piper.

"They'll be great together," said Piper with a dreamy smile.

CHAPTER 18

Piper

After a week of showing themselves in their goddess dresses, Piper felt her power as a soft background buzz, almost but not quite annoying. She continued to give people a place, date, and time to meet someone they could fall in love with. Clara offered advice, and Amy figuratively handed out creativity. They all agreed that human belief made their visions easier to see and more precise.

Brigit never went out again after that first attempt, but the triple goddess continued to go on visiting rounds every afternoon for an entire week. People took photos with them or standing next to Wave Sweeper, and Piper loved helping people find the happiness she had with MacLir. However, the pace they'd set themselves was unsustainable, and the more visits they did, the more requests they received.

The frenzy for Brigit's assistance only intensified the day their local newspaper proclaimed, "MAGICAL CURE FOR CANCER FOUND!" The headline covered the front page of the local paper but, of course, went global. The teenager that Brigit had worked on had doctors reporting that her cancer was disappearing.

"How did you do it?" Amy asked her over breakfast.

Brigit slowly chewed a bite of toast and chugged half her orange juice. "I was thinking about what Clara said, something about hope. And the reason that hope is so powerful is the brain directs it. I'm much better at healing the mind than the body. So I helped her mind use the hope it already had to believe she would be healed."

"Neat… but you fainted, so would that always happen if you tried healing others?"

"I was already tired, so probably not. Although, I'm afraid it won't last. Hope is powerful, but cancer is an unfortunate part of life. I honestly don't know which one will win out."

Piper's anger rose hot when, by the end of that day, reporters showed up clamoring at the door yet again. Clara advised them not to answer but saw the people camped outside were not all reporters. More people came the next day and still more the next. They set up tents or slept in their rental cars. They came from around the world, and all had incurable illnesses.

Meeting in a kitchen furthest from the people and with all the curtains drawn, MacLir said, "It's time to go."

"No!" Piper readjusted Emily on her hip and glared at MacLir. "This is our home. We can't let them force us to leave."

"It's no longer safe here," Lucky pointed out gently. "Those people out there will only have so much patience before they start trying to break in to get healing."

"I can't heal all of them, but I guess I could try to do a few?" asked Brigit.

"No," said Lucky. "We should not have shown them what we can do. They won't be happy unless you help them all. More are arriving every day. I agree with MacLir. It's time to leave."

Amy put her hands on her hips. "I just finished getting

my house exactly as I want, and I think we should wait it out. Don't offer to heal them since I agree that will worsen the mess, but things were going fine last week. If we wait, won't this die down too?"

"Not this time," disagreed Robin. "And we have to keep the safety of everyone in mind. Besides, I miss you. You don't plan to keep leaving so much do you?"

"And if you don't keep leaving to help people," chimed in Lucky, "we'll have even more people camped outside our door."

MacLir turned to Clara. "What wisdom can you give us?"

Clara's eyes were unfocused, then widened in fear. "Everyone duck! Now, now!"

The group dropped to their knees, Piper and MacLir sheltering Emily with their bodies as a boom came from outside, causing windows to shatter and blow inward from the force that landed near the house.

"It's a bomb, everyone out! Get to the ship!" shouted Clara.

Robin held Amy tight as they ran and said, "It's The Voiceless Pure. I'd heard rumors they were gathering bombs but could never find them. They must have seen our house on the news."

Lucky growled. "I'm done with this nonsense. I'm going into the tunnels and stopping this right now."

"I'll come with you," said MacLir, anger deeply lining a face that rarely knew such an emotion.

"No!" Piper said, fearing for him and Lucky. She hugged Emily closer and held her feet in place, putting her several paces behind the group, who stopped to wait for her. "Don't go down there. You could get hurt!"

"We must go, Piper."

From the threat of a bomb hurting Emily to the possibility of MacLir getting killed in the tunnels, it was clear her priorities were skewed. Making plans based on protecting the house as the most critical thing was so wrong. "Fine, we can abandon the house, but come with us, don't leave us alone."

"We can't keep running from the unrest. I'm going with Lucky, and you must get Emily far away. Hurry now, and I'll come to find you later." MacLir gently pushed Piper toward the ship, then turned in the opposite direction without looking back.

As Piper flew the ship up and over the house, she saw MacLir jump off the cliff and disappear into the Otherworld before he hit the waves. She knew it could easily be weeks before they'd see him again with the time difference.

Hazel

Since the speech two days ago, by The Voiceless Pure's pick for High King, she was privately torn about the whole group. Angry, they had tricked her into taking oaths she didn't fully understand. Disappointed that everything she'd been told was a lie. It left a hollow feeling in her stomach that she couldn't fix. Swinging from enraged to miserable left her emotionally exhausted.

Emma didn't understand, and Hazel could not explain. She tried at first. Pointing out the orange armbands, the contradictions, all the things that didn't add up. Emma laughed at her, saying she was worried about nothing, but since the speech, things have changed between them. The first night she slept on the floor of Emma's room. The next night she didn't go home with Emma and slept on the team's common room couch instead.

Everything she had worked toward was fake. All she wanted was a peaceful world with enough food to eat and the sun shining through her windows. It didn't feel like a lot to ask of life, but maybe she was being naive. Was maintaining an honest government and a peaceful civilization so hard? Was it even possible for the Tua De to return to their golden age of heroes?

"Good morning, Hazel," said the team leader, Tua De, in a high-ranking soldier's blue armband.

"Good morning," she replied, as sweet as honey. However she felt inside, she was careful not to show it to her team or leaders. If she could gain his trust, maybe she could find out how to break the binding spell.

For days they practiced their roles in the upcoming war by shifting items from one room to another, then from the tunnels to above-ground bases. In the last few days, they had moved the bombs from the underground to locations world-wide. She had never known how rare her magic was, out of all her people only the few on her team had a variation of it. They'd show her a picture of the place and pointed to it on a map, and she could feel the path to send the item.

By the end of each day, she had a headache but didn't let it show. Instead, she fist-pumped the air and shouted, "We are changing our future!" with the others,

Although, she didn't believe a word of it anymore.

They'd been told today was the final day of work for their team. The remaining bombs had local targets, so instead of carefully moving them, they would be dropping them. This is what terrified her most. It was one thing to move bombs, knowing they would be used later. It was completely differ-ent to know she'd be killing people today. Humans, but still.

During the loud team party last night, she'd managed to speak privately with each of her teammates, sowing doubt in their minds about what would happen after the war. Some simply shrugged her off, others had listened, but now the team seemed more subdued and wary.

"Why is everyone quiet? Be like my perfect little soldier here and buck up!" said the adult team leader, pointing at Hazel as the perfect example. She smiled warmly at him, then turned back to the others, scowling and rolling her eyes, which the team leader could not see. It was a dangerous game if anyone caught her playing both sides, but she didn't know what else to do.

The team leader guided them to the bomb room, a large, low-ceilinged, and well-lit meeting cave without a stage. It had been packed wall to wall with the metal tubes when she'd first glanced at it, but now only fifteen bombs remained. The team leader announced, "Today is your last big task for the war. I have assignments for each of you based on your skill level and will come around to explain them to you."

He started at the opposite end of the room from where Hazel stood, and she knew it might be a while before he got to her. One bomb disappeared, then a second. She fidgeted, shifting from foot to foot and twirling her hair. Three more bombs departed. She traced the logo on the bomb in front of her with a finger. Five more were gone, and she was close enough to hear the team leader giving directions in his low, serious voice. "Make sure you are visualizing well," or "Be sure to get it high enough in the air."

The one side benefit of the whole mess was her completed training in accurately using her power. It was honestly surprising the High Court let so many people run around trying to do magic without teaching them control.

Her mental tangents had lasted through another bomb disappearing. Eleven down, four to go. The girl next to her glanced over and gave her a nervous smile. She tried to smile back but couldn't and finally shrugged.

She watched Emma accepting directions, then focusing all her attention on the bomb. Hazel missed her friend but didn't feel comfortable being with someone who wholeheartedly believed in an organization she now understood was a deception meant to trap them. She still hoped she could get Emma to see the truth before it was too late, but now she needed to focus on herself.

She had planned to ask her parents if they knew how to break the oaths, but Hazel didn't have time to visit with all the training. The team had been promised free time after today's event was over and before their next assignment. She feared that assignment would be a permanent existence as a servant and needed to escape before that happened. Another two bombs were gone.

The team leader spoke with her immediate neighbor and caught Emma staring at her from across the room. They both looked away after the surprised eye contact.

Hazel reached deep into herself and asked an important question she'd been avoiding. Could she kill today? With the oath in place to obey, did she have a choice?

"It's your turn, and I've saved you the best assignment!" She briefly wondered what her pretend role as teacher's pet had gotten her into, then she flipped through her briefing and felt horror slowly run through her. She'd been given the supposed honor of killing MacLir himself, as well as his whole family. The photos of his house showed where she was supposed to drop the bomb, and the map showed it was not far from the kitchen mounds on the south coast of Ireland.

Hazel didn't know MacLir personally, but she'd seen him at the great feast and knew the stories. Drifting to sleep after hearing about one of his adventures, she'd always been awed by his kindness and generosity. She had been healed in Brigit's infirmary and had hero worship of Piper. So how could she blow up their house? What if they were inside?

"Remember, accuracy is key here," her leader said quietly. "It must get high enough to go off on impact and land inside the courtyard, so it will damage all four houses."

Hazel's stomach roiled. She had pictured blowing up some random human government building full of corrupt politicians, something she could explain away to herself later. Instead, she knew there was an infant in MacLir's household besides Piper and Brigit, and they had done nothing wrong.

She knew she'd been quiet too long, so she pretended concentration by going over each piece of paper in the folder a third time. Afterward, she put both hands on each side of the cold metal tube.

"You will send this bomb to MacLir's house and drop it in the courtyard right now." A direct order from a superior. She felt the magic of the oath crackle over her like static. She closed her eyes and pictured flowing down the map, seeing the house on the coastal cliff, seeing the courtyard. The bomb dissolved under her fingertips, reappearing in her mind's eye directly over the garden from the photo. When it landed, it would destroy everything.

She still gripped the bomb as it hovered in the air. She pushed it when letting go, hard enough that it went careening off course to land in a nearby field she'd seen on the edge of one of the photos. It was closer to the house than she would have liked, but she was sure it had not knocked down any walls.

The team leader smiled at her when she opened her eyes, but his smile faded as energy crackled along her arms. The oath to kill herself if she disobeyed an order pushed to the front of her mind. So, she walked over and pulled the knife from the belt slung around their leader's hips.

The oath was forcing her actions, and Hazel met Emma's eyes as she tried to keep the knife away from her throat. Realizing what was going on, Emma raced up and grabbed Hazel's arm to help her pull the knife away.

"Stop!" ordered the team leader. "She must have disobeyed for the spell to take hold. Emma, let her finish her task."

Emma ignored him, and her disobedience crackled along her own arms, but it loosened the spell's hold. When other team members joined in, grabbing Hazel's arm and one boy even trying to pry the knife loose, the spell wobbled in her mind.

Trying to think of other ways to disobey, Hazel used her free hand to rip off her armband, which loosened the spell further, and the others sensed that and joined in. Soon fifteen orange armbands littered the ground, and all fifteen team members were covered in the tingly blue lightning. During the protest, their handler continuously yelled at them to stop, giving them orders that strengthened the spell, but it only served to balance their group's disobedience.

Hazel wondered how long they could hold out before she died by her own hand, or that of the team leader, when the doors to the cave burst open behind her, and she heard a voice demand, "What is going on here?"

CHAPTER 19

Tamlin

"They've decided a worldwide elimination spell might not make it across the water. So, they've deployed teams to eliminate humans and half-magics on every continent and large island," said the spy Tamlin trusted. It was clear now the generals were playing their own game.

Tamlin stood still in an impromptu communication command center in the library of one of the High Court's member's houses. He had sent away anyone who might spy for the generals and retained only a few people he'd come to trust in his limited time here. He missed his team from the Underwater Kingdom, but he would have to do without them.

He wished he was more disappointed by the news the generals had betrayed him but felt he should have acknowledged their behavior sooner. He was more upset by the mass extinction of humans that was about to take place. "When is this happening? How much time do we have?"

His spy considered for a moment. "All the spells are still set to begin after the second wave of bombs. The first wave is starting to go out now... so... maybe two hours at most?"

The spells he'd authorized, however unwillingly, were localized non-blood magic spells that would be much like the bombs, with an effective radius. So, the timing was the same, but the spells had been switched without his approval. Almost making the bombs pointless. Almost. The first wave would take out their magical enemies. MacLir and his allies, the current High Court, and other creatures might oppose them later.

The deeper he got into the war, the less he liked it. Planning hypotheticals in human pajamas while eating tarts was one thing, but people would start dying at any moment now, and it was his fault. His father had failed to keep away from the humans. He knew they were people, like the Tua De, and it finally hit him that he might have been told other lies. Lies about the sea god with his kind, beautiful eyes. Or even about the current High Court's corruptness. Or perhaps the biggest lie of all, that Tamlin was High King when in reality he was little more than a figurehead.

Another messenger rushed in, dropped a written note at his table, and rushed back out again. Tamlin caught his breath at the handwriting on the outside of the letter. Sam. The message was short. "Our team is here. Meet me at the tarts."

Tamlin smiled at the thinly veiled code for the kitchen. Sam was the only person he'd introduced to the pastry chef, and they were the only two who knew about his sweet tooth. So, Sam must have known he'd seek out the local kitchen looking for dessert.

Wondering when he'd be able to leave the command post, he called himself ten kinds of fool. This was no command post or communication post, for that matter. No one had left him a communicator. None of the generals were here, nothing. He'd been kept out of the way and had been too blind to their lies to see. Standing to leave, he paused when another messenger burst in.

"The sea god is raging through the tunnels looking for the people responsible for bombing his house. He's already found the dead High Court and is headed this way. You need to run, sir." The man took his own advice, fleeing from the study and outer doors into the tunnels.

Tamlin heard the distant roar of moving water, something he'd never heard in this house before, and jumped into action, his chair landing on the floor behind him. He followed the messenger without bothering to take anything with him. Reaching the left fork in the tunnel toward the kitchen, just as he saw a wall of water coming down the right fork, caused him to pick up his pace. He ran faster than he ever thought he would need to. Ignoring the mud splattered on his jumpsuit, he slid down the wet tunnels.

The adrenaline rush carried him to the kitchens, where he turned a corner to find Sam waiting for him. The other boy was chatting with Ginger, and his team stood alert behind them. His eyes met Sam's from across the room, and he was frozen in place by uncertainty. Tamlin swallowed hard, the last time they'd been together flashing through his mind, holding hands, the one short kiss that was over too quickly.

Sam was glorious in human clothes, he noticed. Tight black jeans and a peacoat over a light blue button-up shirt. Not sure what to say or how to proceed when all he wanted to do was hold Sam close, Tamlin stood rigid.

Until Sam took a step forward, then another. He opened his arms wide, and Tamlin rushed into them. Their lips met with perfect timing, and neither could be sure who started the passionate kiss. Their team cheered while Ginger clapped. "Let's never get separated again," said Sam when they had to stop for air.

Tamlin laughed and nodded his agreement, too overcome for words, as Sam led him over to the fireplace and settled him with a cup of tea. Then, sitting on the arm of the chair next to Tamlin, Sam said, "I thought we'd be waiting for you a lot longer since you are busy leading an army."

The warm tea soothed the tightness in Tamlin's throat, and he chuckled. "Oh, not me. I'm not in charge. Not really, anyway." The bitterness in his tone surprised him, but everything he'd prepared for was pointless. Those old generals had needed someone inspiring, and he'd believed every word they'd told him, like his now-dead foster brother.

"Not in charge?" asked Ginger. "Of what? When were you ever in charge?"

"I'm The Pure's High King, or I was until today. Who did you think I was?"

"One of the sad refugees from the boat. We housed many people who fled the underwater caves, and they all wore jumpsuits and armbands like yours. Someone told me that the embroidery on your armband meant you were Cian's son... but we weren't told you were part of the madness going on with that cult rebellion. You and I are supposed to be enemies, you know."

"Not anymore. I need to stop them, but I don't know how. The first wave of bombs has been sent, but we could still stop some of the second wave. Maybe. More importantly, we have to stop the spells." He outlined the problem as quickly as he could while still being thorough. That teams of fifteen had been scattered over the earth with either blood magic spells to kill humans or bombs to take out any of the magic community that might cause problems.

"Can't we simply find one of the communicators, and you can call it off?" asked Sam.

"Nope, I was only ever a figurehead. I never had a communications device. The generals in our home and their contacts here were always running things. I just didn't realize it in time."

"A figurehead," mused Ginger. "The plotters know that, and you know that, but do the teams know it?"

"Of course!" said Sam, jumping to his feet. "As a figurehead, you still have the power to stop everything. So, all we need is a communicator. Is there a local team nearby?"

"Yes, I know where to get one," said Tamlin, placing his teacup gently on the table and leading his team out of the kitchen.

He tried to hold in his agitation that the second wave of bombs was probably starting, but the important thing would be to get to a communicator before the spells started, so that's what he had to focus on.

Arriving in the bomb storage room he'd seen during a brief tour, he hoped the team had not left after their assignment. He burst in, the double doors swinging wide, to find a scene of what could only be described as chaos. One girl held a knife and the whole team was glowing blue. Hands-on hips, he demanded, "What is going on here?"

A soldier in a blue armband rushed up to him, "Oh sir, it's a good thing you are here. I have a whole team rebelling against the oath. I'll need you as a backup to get them under control again."

"Me, what can I do?"

"All the individual team oaths were tied together and bound to the highest authority, and since you are High King, that must be you."

Tamlin reached out with his power that could usually only sense minds and was hit with the turmoil of the group grappling with each other. They were fighting a spell laid on them that he felt indirectly linked to him. He broke the connection to the oath, and all fifteen boys and girls collapsed.

The soldier gasped. "Sir, you broke it! You accidently broke the spell. Now they are free!"

"It wasn't an accident. Everyone should be free," said Tamlin. "Free to do as they please, eat what they want, and love who they love."

The soldier backed away, shock on his face. "Get his communicator," Tamlin told his team. They surrounded the man and ripped his belt off, despite his screams and protests. When they had what they wanted, he scrambled toward the door, but four of Tamlin's team held him while another handed over the all-important communicator. The most important thing in the world right now.

"Calling all teams. I repeat this is a message for all teams from your High King. Stand down. Do not proceed as planned. Stand down. Traitors in the ranks gave some of you misguided instructions. Do not do anything until you hear from me. Notify your direct commanding officers that you received this message, but take no further instructions for action from anyone. I repeat, stand down."

"Thank you, sir, for saving me," said a plump girl with a reddish tint to her blond hair. The Tua De girl wore a brown jumpsuit. So, a half-magic, he thought to himself, recognizing the symbolism.

"What was going on?" he asked.

"They had us take an oath of obedience. If we failed to obey, we would have to kill ourselves."

Tamlin sighed. He'd never authorized anything like that and, in fact, had never even heard of it. He mentally reached out again and found the residual feel of the spell. Closing his eyes to concentrate better, he followed the sensation to an active knot that sent spider web thin lines out to countless other similar teams. He tugged the knot, loosening it until it broke, disconnecting all the oaths to the power source.

"I didn't know about that before today, but I've just broken the oaths for all the teams who took them," explained Tamlin. "Your team rebelled against the oath today. Why?"

"I refused to kill MacLir and his family. My team actually assisted in trying to save me from the oath."

Tamlin felt a weight lift that at least some people had survived the start of the war. He was starting to feel like MacLir might be someone he'd like to know better and was glad of the chance. Raising his voice to include the whole group, Tamlin said, "My team is also turning away from the schemes of war. Would your team join us to continue finding a way to stop the destruction?"

A cheer went up from the orange armband team, and an answering cheer came from his own team of blues. Now he had more help, but what to do with it? The next most pressing matter would be to ensure the generals didn't override his stop order, but he wasn't sure where to find them. The terrified handler whimpered from behind him, giving him an idea.

He ordered one of his men with hypnotic powers to interrogate the man. They learned the location of the secretive actual communication command center but found only a single aide on arriving. Repeating the interrogation process, they discovered the generals were angry about Tamlin calling off their careful plans honed over decades and had decided to take it out MacLir. Spies had confirmed the bomb intended for him had gone off course and that his family had returned to their home.

Tamlin sent one person to find and warn the sea god of the general's intentions and led the rest of his small army to the nearest transport tunnel. While waiting for his turn to go through, he edged up to Sam, linking pinkies and giving the boy a kiss on the cheek. Sam grinned, then pushed him into the transporter before following after.

CHAPTER 20

Clara

"Every window in the house is dark," sent Piper.

"It was afternoon when we left, and there was no need to turn lights on with that many windows," snorted Amy.

Clara nodded her agreement but kept silent, watching the outside yard in the dim twilight, examining the mess from the fleeing campers and the bomb debris for any movement.

Having spent a week on Wave Sweeper in cramped proximity with too many worried and frustrated people, Clara's idea was to return to the house to spread out a little. Her home's residence on the far side of the destroyed field still had all its glass windows intact. She'd requested multiple guest bedrooms be included in the building design for her children and their friends to visit. It would be enough room for everyone to stay temporarily while they waited for MacLir and Lucky to return.

They'd parked Wave Sweeper a little way off to watch the area first. The entire property was empty and quiet. Completely abandoned by the media and public.

"It's so eerie," sent Amy. "Are you sure we should go back?"

"All the bombs happened on the same day. Now there's been nothing for almost a week," pointed out Clara.

"That means all the bombs had to have been sent within an hour of each other. They could send more any minute if they were being sent from the Otherworld. For MacLir, it probably hasn't even been a full day since he left us." The worry rolling off Piper was enough to twist Clara's stomach, and she was already on edge.

She needed time alone. At least enough to regroup and recharge her mental battery. Time with people exhausted her, even people she liked, and this last week of waiting had been unbearably stressful being cooped up. So instead of acknowledging Piper, or her misgivings, she whispered aloud for everyone to hear, "It looks quiet. Let's go."

They ventured closer, parking Wave Sweeper in the interior courtyard, and watched. Minutes ticked by, and when nothing moved and no sounds came from the house, they put down the ramp for a potential quick retreat and dared go inside with Robin leading the way.

Accomplished at pushing through mental strain, Clara flipped on the kitchen lights and began making a light dinner for everyone. If she could make it through the next half hour, she planned to lock herself in her suite with a bag full of snacks and stay there all day tomorrow. A day of silence, if she could get one, always reset her brain and relaxed the built-up tension in her shoulders.

The tired group lined up at her kitchen counter bar, watching her cook, adding to her anxiety. She could feel them tracking her every movement and wanted to run away. Arranging omelets onto plates, she turned around with one in each hand to deliver them to hungry people at the bar and gasped. An omelet slipped to the floor as her hands went slack. "Behind you!" she sent to Amy and Piper.

They both twirled around in alarm to see what she was looking at. At least thirty men in green armbands streamed in, making the large kitchen feel cramped. Tall men with brown hair, green eyes, and green armbands. The young among them each carried swords or guns. The older Tua De had no weapons, but Clara felt that made them more dangerous. Almost as if they thought they were powerful enough that non-magical weapons were inferior.

The shadows in the doorways moved rapidly as more of the enemy filed in to line up behind one man. Clara was shocked to see his proud face lined with wrinkles, something she'd never seen on a Tua De before. Silver was threaded through his hair, and his eyes were greener than Lucky's.

"We don't want to fight!" said Clara loudly.

"Don't worry," said the old man, "there will be minimal fighting. Mostly only killing."

Brigit went pale when she was finally in a position to see their new guests. "Cian!" she exclaimed. "I… I thought you were dead."

"You would have liked that, wouldn't you? You and MacLir, and the rest of the High Court. You all turned against me! You banned me from my home and from the nightly feast. In taking away my immortality, you assumed I would die slowly instead of by your hands. But I survived, and now it's you who will die. Don't worry, though. It will be a much quicker death than you intended for me."

"We didn't—" began Brigit, but he cut her off.

"These stalwart men around me are the children of the men you banished. They are ready to finish what you started." Clara looked at the glares of the old men. Not as elderly as Cian, but indeed older than the youthful faces of the group. She'd always seen the Tua De as ageless but remembered something Piper had mentioned about MacLir sharing his magic Pig with them when they were conquered. So apparently, they could age and die. Not only that but these children and grandchildren had been raised by their parents to hate everything–the system and people that banned them from living where they felt at home. Generational hatred was some of the most powerful.

Cian continued his monologue about MacLir, saying the ban was all his fault, and Clara began to plan. The kitchen knife block was only one step away from her. Clara decided her weapon of choice would be the still hot cast iron skillet behind her.

If they could keep him talking, maybe help would come. Or, at least the group would have recovered from shock enough to fight, and she'd have more time to plan. She decided Amy was the most chatty of them all and sent, "Amy, keep him ranting. He likes talking about himself, so ask him how he stayed alive."

With the right balance of fear and curiosity, Amy asked, "So, how did you stay alive when the rest of your supporters died?"

"I finally convinced my contacts to send me enough of the Pig to continue living and to preserve my sons to lead our armies."

"Why not lead them yourself?" she continued.

"I knew I would not be accepted in the Irish tunnels as the new High King, not right away. So, I sent my first son to pave the way and picked a foster son to create a likable figurehead. Then, when the time was near, I disguised myself as one of the generals. Not that it mattered. If I can't be High King and we are forced to go into hiding again, we'll be happy to know we got revenge on those who banned us. I've already killed the High Court members, so now all I need is MacLir… and you, Brigit. I'm happy to wipe out MacLir's family and allies too."

Lucky popped into the kitchen with his unbeatable sword, The Answerer. It glimmered dangerously under the bright kitchen lights, but he lowered it slightly when he recognized who was speaking. "Father?"

Cian inclined his head toward the son he'd abandoned.

"I'm not happy with you," said Lucky.

"I don't care what you think, half-magic," Cian replied coldly.

MacLir burst in from the front room, dripping wet and breathing heavily. "Cian, I demand you leave my house right now."

"That won't be happening," he told MacLir with a dark chuckle, turning to his men behind. "Kill everyone!"

The battle began with too many deafening sounds, from stillness to action, silence to pandemonium. Clara knocked over the knife block, and the makeshift weapons went skittering toward Amy and Piper. "Get Emily upstairs," Clara sent the other women, "and take a knife with you." She then turned to grab the frying pan and spun back around in time to deflect a half-hearted sword swing.

Feeling a vision coming on, she tried to push it away. Not now, she told the magic, but it came anyway. She ducked again to give herself time to come out of the trance and saw herself tell the Tua De in front of her, "Choose your friends carefully." She didn't pay nearly as much attention to the words this time as to the actions. His next sword swing would catch her in the arm, but now she'd seen which way to move to avoid it. Shifting away from the danger, she slammed her eight-pound skillet into his shoulder and heard a crunch. He went down hard, his sword clattering to the tiles.

Picking up his sword, she slid it across the kitchen bar. "Robin! Use this!" As a distraction, he kicked his opponent in the knee and switched his steak knife out for the sword.

Briefly surveying the room, she saw MacLir punching people, trying to make his way through the layers of protection around Cian, who was smugly watching the scene. Brigit was assisting MacLir, putting people to sleep one at a time when she could get into contact with their skin. Lucky protected her by wounding people and keeping her moving forward.

Robin was guarding the retreat of the girls, but he was getting overwhelmed, and Clara ran to join him, her stomach dropping when she saw reinforcements streaming in through the other side of the kitchen. A dozen or more girls and boys younger than her own children, but with fists in the air, they gave a loud roar in unison, then forced their way into the fight.

Tamlin

The lock gave way as Tamlin kicked at the door. He didn't have time to look for another entrance. He could hear the battle raging nearby. Leading his team and the other team through the dark interior, they headed toward the only light in the house.

Reaching the attack, he could see it was not going well for MacLir's family and instantly joined in as backup. He called his team to stop everyone with a green armband and began putting people to sleep. Feeling for the closest minds, he quieted their fevered brains into slumber. Getting close to MacLir, he hesitated when he saw the goal of the sea god.

Cian.

The elderly Tua De had not seen Tamlin's team yet, and his foster father's eyes glowed triumph as he watched the sea god fail to get near him. In Tamlin's pause, he saw his team tackling the younger fighters and the kinetic Ireland team throwing kitchen objects at older fighters. When Cian was hit with a banana, it jolted him out of his single-minded glee. He opened his eyes to what else was happening in the fray around him.

Tamlin picked up his offense again, and MacLir glanced over at him when people began to drop around them faster than Brigit could accomplish with her healing sleep. Cian's eyes widened as the crowd thinned, darting for the doorway and up the stairs.

"No!" shouted MacLir, and with a growl, took off after him.

Tamlin let them go, deciding the best thing he could do was calm the situation downstairs, but he sensed something. Actively feeling for it, he identified the oath spell similar to the one that bound the teams to him. This one was not connected to him, but it was the same type of magic.

Now that he'd pinpointed the sensation of the spell, he noted it in all of the young people he was knocking out, but none of the older generation. Tamlin had begun to suspect what that meant, but for now, he needed to put the safety of his team first and, second, make sure the family they were rescuing was safe. Eventually, some other day, he could find out why the man he'd called father had lied so much.

Tamlin collapsed on a bar stool when everyone was down. The teams he was leading were cheering for their quick victory, but he'd never used his power so much at once, and his dizzy head could have used a headrest to lean against. Instead, Tamlin found his support in Sam's chest. His love came to stand beside him, pulling Tamlin in and settling his head against the warm silky shirt. "Are you doing okay?" Sam asked.

"Better now," said Tamlin, his smile evident in his tone.

"I have a surprise for you," began Sam. "It's a—" His breath caught in his throat as he was cut off by the noise of screaming and gunshots from upstairs.

CHAPTER 21

Piper

The knife felt wrong in Piper's hand. She was finally used to cutting vegetables, but she held the knife carefully angled down. Then, balancing a screaming Emily on one hip, with the kitchen knife raised defensively in front of her, she backed toward the stairs. Amy was already on the first step, and the only person who came near them was threatened by Vixen's sharp teeth and quickly retreated to find a different opponent for fighting. "Go!" Vixen sent, running beside her as they crossed the hall and sprinted up the stairs.

Piper wanted to help but knew she needed to get Emily away from the attack. MacLir would know what to do, and Lucky was fearsome with his unbeatable sword. She convinced herself they would be okay while she did what she was told and ran for cover with Amy to guard her.

At the top of the stairs, Amy waited in the dark. "Which way?" she asked. "Where should we hide?"

A hallway stretched to the left with five doors on one side and a solid wall of darkened windows opposite, letting in the faint moonlight. Piper calmed Emily while opening the first door to discover a bathroom. The next two doors were both small bedrooms. Ignoring Amy's pacing, she tried another door, finding a narrow stairway up to the third floor.

"If it was me, I'd expect someone I was chasing to keep running up higher, so let's go hide in the last door," sent Piper.

Amy agreed, leaving the door to the upper level cracked in hopes of misdirecting anyone who might have followed them. So instead, they let the moonlight guide them to the last door. Once inside, Amy flipped on the light. "No! Turn that off. They'll know exactly where we are!" sent Piper.

"Sorry," muttered Amy before sending, "Sorry, I wasn't thinking. But we can't just stand here in the dark."

Piper called out her hand light, the waxing moon challenging to see as she clutched the knife. She dropped the kitchen knife on the dresser and raised her hand to look around. Although she'd never been in it, it must be Clara's bedroom, similar to her bedroom, which had an adjoining bathroom.

"Come on," she sent. Emily burbled in her ear, Vixen padded next to her, and Amy followed behind. Passing through Clara's private things felt odd without her here, but Piper knew the older woman wouldn't mind since it was for their safety.

Closing everyone into the bathroom, she locked the door behind them and prepared to wait. She was furious that more waiting would be required. She'd been waiting for MacLir all week, seen him briefly in the doorway, and now this. More waiting for her safety. She wondered if she should have stayed to fight but imagined using the knife to cut someone's skin open and almost gagged. Besides, what if she missed and they didn't? She wasn't happy about the waiting but knew it was for the good of her family, so it didn't bear dwelling on.

Swallowing hard a few times to settle her stomach, she tried to think of a distraction and heard a roar of voices below her. "What do you think that was?" she sent to Amy.

She could see Amy shrug in the soft glow of the moons in their hands. Emily was mesmerized by the glow, silent as she focused on trying to pick up the light globe like a ball and continuously failing.

Piper wanted to send the question to Clara and ask if everyone was doing okay but was worried about distracting the woman. An idea burned through her mind, so quick and fierce that she knew it had come from outside herself. Because of their connection, something told her she could see through Clara's eyes. For only an instant, she wondered if some past part of the triple goddess was connecting to her.

About to put the new information into action, she hesitated. If tramping through Clara's room was an invasion of privacy, what would she think about Piper in her head? But what if it helped? What if they could leave Emily here with Vixen, and go assist the rest of the group? What if MacLir needed her? Better to apologize later than try to contact Clara now for permission, and possibly distract her.

Reaching out like a sending, she instead followed the message toward Clara. A shiver went through her body, then she was blinded by the bright kitchen. Her actual eyes were fine, but her mind was not ready for the shift from dark to light. It was disorienting to feel her body still sitting on the bathroom floor but watching what Clara saw.

The battle was mostly won. Somehow reinforcements had arrived, fighting around MacLir, and people dropped two at a time without even being touched. She could see Cian's anger and confusion at the turn of events etched into his face. He retreated a step, then raced for the stairs with MacLir at his heels.

"Piper!" sent Clara. "What in the world are you doing? Stop that, it feels weird." Clara pushed, and Piper found herself back in the bathroom, having never physically left.

"Amy, Cian's is coming up here," sent Piper.

"What? How do you know? What do we do?" Amy was rocking in place with pent-up agitation, and Piper wondered if she should have at least left Amy below to fight.

They froze when they heard the bedroom door open and footsteps coming toward them. The steps slowed when MacLir's voice whispered, "Piper, are you in there? I heard voices."

Amy and Piper released a breath of relief, and Piper unlocked the door. As she cracked it open, a shout from MacLir and then two gunshots sounded, and the door swung wide as MacLir crashed backward into it and landed on the floor.

Piper peaked out the open door to see Lucky hit Cian on the head from behind, both outlined in moonlight. With the threat taken care of, she flipped on the light and saw MacLir, with two bleeding wounds in his chest. He was dead.

Emily had begun wailing at the booming sound of the gunshots, but her infant lungs could not rival Piper's wild screaming.

Piper

It was still dark out the porthole window of her room in Wave Sweeper, but a grayness to the sky implied dawn was not far off. The fresh blood-free shirt she'd put on was all she came in here to do, but she didn't feel strong enough to return to the deck where Lucky and Brigit were preparing to carry MacLir's body down to his island.

Lucky's voice from earlier replayed in her head for the millionth time. "Elementals are nature spirits given form by human imagination," said Lucky. "In theory, he can't die."

The pig was reborn on the island every time he died, so Lucky's theory was that MacLir should too. Piper didn't feel like it would work, but instead, she chose to focus on the hope that Lucky had given her.

"Are you coming?" she sent to Flutter.

"Do I usually follow you to the big litter box by the water?" asked Flutter dryly, and she went back to cleaning her ears with a wet, curled paw.

Vixen bumped her hand, pushing her big soft head into Piper's thigh. "Cheeky cat. Let's go," she added in a subdued voice that didn't make it easy for Piper to cling to hope as she padded out of the cabin into the chilly morning air.

"Hurry. Pig appears at dawn, so will MacLir," said Lucky, his puffy eyes contradicting his confident tone. Brigit reached for his hand and squeezed it before descending Wave Sweeper's ramp. Lucky followed her, carrying MacLir's body down in the waves. They watched it float away into the dark water, as MacLir would have wanted, then sat by the hut to wait for dawn. All was silent except for the soft lap of the low tide on the rock pool. The gray skies gave way to blue. Finally, a yellow line appeared on the horizon, growing until the sky was yellow, streaked with pink.

The higher the sun rose, the lower Piper's heart sank.

Finally, the orange ball of light was high enough above the horizon to strike the ocean, and a path of light was created across the water in a line directly to the island. At that moment, winds swirled around the island with the sound of roaring waves. The wind blew, out on the water, making a water spout that slowly came back to the island along the path of light. It splashed away when it reached the sand, revealing a familiar form.

"MacLir!" squeaked Piper happily, running toward the naked sea god. She took one running leap into MacLir's arms and fell to the sand at his feet when he didn't catch her. He looked down at her and blinked twice. Then, turned and began walking to the ocean.

"Manannán, my friend," said Lucky, standing in front of MacLir. The form shifted around Lucky and continued to the water. Lucky shrugged, "He's new, or at least this body is. I don't think he remembers us."

"Or, we might need to help him remember," commented Brigit.

"Stop him!" said Piper tearfully. "If he reaches the water, we may never see him again!"

Lucky's face went white with realization. He flashed away, and while he was gone, Vixen slowed MacLir down by jumping around in front of him. By the time Lucky returned with his sword, MacLir was knee-deep in the waves. Lucky pounded the back of MacLir's head with the hilt, as he'd done to Cian hours earlier.

"What if you'd killed him doing that!" cried Piper, remembering Cian's lifeless body in the hallway.

Lucky shrugged again. "Then we would start over tomorrow morning."

Piper shuddered, considering waiting through another dawn for another MacLir to appear, but had to admit he was right. Since MacLir was so much stronger than Lucky, she couldn't think of anything else that would have stopped him.

She helped pull the new MacLir up the beach to the hut's door, and Brigit hovered hands over his head. Piper didn't breathe as Brigit's eyebrows lowered over her closed eyes. She sat back in the sand with a sigh, ignoring how dirty and tangled her silver dress was becoming.

"I'll bet he can still speak to sea creatures," she said, "but as far as I can tell, his mind is empty, unlearned like an infant."

"Can you make him remember?" Piper whispered.

"His memories are not in this body, which is MacLir only physically. So he won't be the MacLir we know unless those memories are returned to this living form."

Despair swamped Piper and tears made her vision blurry. Her mind whirled with a future she didn't want to be part of, a life without MacLir. No one to wake up to, no one to raise their daughter with, no one to make her laugh. "The sea… the sea…" she muttered, rocking back and forth.

A panic attack and a meltdown were fighting for control of her mind, but one thought kept pushing in. The sea. He'd told her once that he was part of the sea. "I have an idea! Would the water remember?" As soon as the words were out of her mouth, she regretted saying anything. It was a dumb idea, her despair told her.

However, Brigit jolted upright at the suggestion. Running directly into the waves, she held her hands lightly on the top of the water as if it was a living thing she could heal, then called, "Yes! The sea kept his memories. Bring him over here."

With Vixen bounding around them like a puppy, Lucky and Piper dragged MacLir back in the same trench they'd made when bringing him up the beach and laid him partway in the water. Vixen's enthusiasm was catching, and Piper's stomach fluttered with hope.

"He would have reabsorbed the memories eventually, I think, maybe," said Brigit, "but this will be faster." Then, with one hand in the water and one hand on MacLir's forehead, she said, "AWAKE."

MacLir's eyes popped open, and he struggled against Piper and Lucky, trying to sit up.

"REMEMBER," said Brigit loudly. As the word echoed away, the blank expression left MacLir's face. He went still and looked up at the three faces crowding around him.

"Piper," he breathed softly.

CHAPTER 22

Tamlin

The day was long, made longer since Tamlin could only watch as every Tuatha Dé Danann from both realms passed through the large meeting room. He'd somewhat unwillingly been part of the blood magic spell that brought them all here. Everyone was drawn to the closest thing they had as a leader. Now all he had to do was sit here, a flame attracting the moths.

He'd already examined the massive ocean-themed tapestry scenes lining the walls of MacLir's sea cave throne room. MacLir himself had shown Tamlin what was behind a blue door in the only tapestry gap, a simple bed, and some shelves. Indirect light came in through the large front opening, and he could hear high tide waves crashing on the rocks, though they were out of sight. The rest of the light came from several holes in the ceiling, letting in bright rays of sunlight that highlighted the otherwise invisible dust motes floating through the room.

With nothing else to occupy his time, all Tamlin could do was watch as his people streamed endlessly in and out of the room, tracking mud on the huge, round, blue-ish green rug. He sat on a distressingly painful piece of metal that he'd been told was called a folding chair. Brigit oversaw several stations with groups of healers working together, all in a circle of similar chairs with one person sitting on the ground in the middle. The healers were sorting the minds of everyone who came in, untangling a mess of brainwashing mixed with oath spells to return people to a calm, open state of mind.

MacLir also watched the proceedings, from his throne, with Lucky sitting next to him. Although they didn't seem to mind their seats as much as Tamlin, they both remained grim, but maybe they were simply as bored as he was.

He glanced uneasily over at the growing number of people who were not persuaded into the war. The temporarily swayed were released back to their everyday lives, but the instigators were being detained. Those who fully believed in what they were doing based on the half-truths they'd been told growing up. Most of their parents had been banished for causing trouble with the same ideals they were following, and it would not end well for them either.

Brigit had checked Tamlin's mind at the start of the day, so he was the first one released from the distorted views of the cult. His father's influence peeled away to let him see how he'd been manipulated. The spells of confusion and obedience removed showed him the love he felt for his foster father was fake as well. It all left him feeling shaky and ill. The lies were obvious now, but he'd been young and trusting. At least he'd learned a few valuable lessons, like how to lead and who to trust in the future.

Sam. He trusted Sam. Putting his hands in the plush pockets of the jacket Sam had given him, he luxuriated in the feel of the thick, soft fabric they used inside the pockets. This jacket was so different from the stylish rough wool on the outside of Sams's peacoat. He smiled down at his newest pair of socks from Ginger. It was nice to have friends that knew his name and understood what he liked. His fingers itched for the sketchbook and pencils that Sam had also given him. He'd already filled countless pages with clothing designs and couldn't wait to try making them.

The clothes of the many people wandering in gave him so much inspiration. They wore a mix of clothes from every era except the half-magics from the human realm. They wore current fashions like what he'd seen on the most recent captives in the Underwater Kingdom they'd left behind. He didn't miss his old home, old beliefs, or his old wardrobe. The hours slipped by, and his head filled with all the fabrics and styles he wanted to add to his design book, yet people kept coming.

He had no idea there were so many Tuatha Dé Danann in the world, well over a thousand, and by the end of the day, dozens of rebels lay snoozing in the corner. Tamlin had put them to sleep rather than try to have them guarded or deal with escape attempts. When the last Tua De was checked, Brigit's healer crew staggered out the door for a much-needed rest. Only the four of them remained to decide the fate of many.

Brigit opened a folding chair to sit by Lucky, and Tamlin dragged his uncomfortable metal atrocity closer to MacLir. After a brief tension-filled silence, Brigit finally spoke. "We can't ban them from the island again. They have even more rage than their parents against humans. So, we can't turn them loose on the world either."

"I don't want them caged for the rest of their life," pointed out MacLir. "It's cruel and pointless."

"Do you want them executed instead?" asked Lucky quietly, slouching unhappily in his folding chair.

"No," said MacLir. "They've been lied to and whipped into a frenzy. It's not completely their fault."

"Other people accepted the truth and moved on," said Lucky.

"These are passionate people," said Brigit. "Their minds are strong. For them, the reality they were told is their truth, and they cling to that belief."

"So, we don't have another choice. Just because they didn't die in battle doesn't mean they still can't die now," said Lucky. Tamlin noticed his tone didn't match his words, though. The past king slouched further in his chair, putting wrinkles in otherwise impeccable custom, fitted clothes.

Brigit, usually so calm, tensed her shoulders and glared at Lucky. "They can't be killed for their beliefs!"

"They are not," he replied. "They'd be given a traitor's death for acting on those beliefs in a way that recently killed thousands. Not only humans, but we lost people too."

Brigit glanced down and away but said clearly, "I bring life and healing, not death. I don't condone killing them."

"I don't want them locked up," repeated MacLir.

Lucky rolled his eyes dramatically, "Well, that brings us back to banishment, which has always been used in the past but will not work this time."

Tamlin watched the three of them argue but could tell they held no real annoyance at each other. It seemed like a conversation they'd had before and were no closer to agreeing on. He remembered the healers earlier, releasing people from spells and distorted beliefs. Tamlin wondered if something similar might be done for the flawed views that led some of his people to violence. "How bad are their minds? Could they perhaps be… talked to? Helped? In some way? Maybe explain to them what went wrong so they could understand?" asked Tamlin, hope rising in his chest.

"No… it's become part of their culture. It's how they view the world," Brigit shook her head. "However, MacLir, what about your Cloak of Destiny? That doesn't change their personality, but could make them forget their hatred and resentment."

Tamlin knew of the Cloak. In his nightly reading, he'd studied and memorized his father's carefully written histories. The Cloak could change a person's fate for good or bad, depending on the intentions of the person wielding it. For a moment, hesitation curled through him that a monster like MacLir was the keeper of the Cloak, but he remembered what he'd be told was a lie, and the mistrust dissipated like morning mist.

Every time his old training reared its head, he squashed it. Each time, it was easier to do, but it still felt hard, even after he'd broken through some of the coercion spells in his mind before Brigit's help. Although it was his idea to try talking them out of their beliefs, Tamlin privately agreed with Brigit. They would need to find a magical solution to the problem caused by magic.

Lucky sat up with a broad smile at the suggestion of the new solution. He disappeared with a slight pop, something Tamlin was still not used to seeing. He'd read about the gods and the powers given to them by human belief, but the open use of such powerful magic would take getting used to. So even though he was braced for it, he still stared when Lucky returned with a mass of fabric over one arm.

Tamlin gasped at the rich dark green shades merging together and could not resist reaching out to stroke the woolen texture. "It's beautiful," he told MacLir, who smiled at Tamlin's shock and joy.

Draping the cloak over his bare chest, MacLir fastened it with the clasp, and the bottom hem flowed around his feet, hiding his brown side-laced pants from view. Marching to the nearest shaft of light coming down from the ceiling, he twirled the cape around in a sweeping arc. The magic activated, turning the wool almost metallic, and causing every rainbow hue to appear and shimmer, nearly blinding in the dim cave. Sparkles bounced off the clock colors, creating tiny reflections of light dancing on the tapestries.

Tamlin was so mesmerized by the sight he almost didn't hear MacLir ask him to wake the group. When he understood the request, he pulled them all out of sleep, doing as much as possible, being quick instead of careful. The men and women, disoriented from waking from their unnatural sleep, looked up at the shimmery cloak in dazed amazement.

MacLir stood in front of them, and as soon as all eyes were on him, he announced, "Clear your heart of rage. Let go of the culture that tells you to hate. Embrace new ideas. Trust your own instinct of what is right and wrong. Go now and live happily through the power of the Cloak of Destiny!" When he finished his gift to them for a better future, he grabbed the edge of his cloak and swung it around again in one big curve away from the group that caused it to fade back to its dark green color.

Piper

Amy leaned against the interior of her front door, eyes wide and breathing heavy. Reporters crowded around outside, their shouts for an interview clearly heard, even from the far side of the room where Piper sat on the couch entertaining Emily with a ring of rubber toy keys.

"I can't deal with any more of this. Not even one little bit," declared Amy.

"Good, I'm glad you agree, " said MacLir. "And now, with that settled… I want to talk about the future. We are too public, and it's become dangerous. So I feel we should leave the house and fade into legend."

"No," gasped Piper. "Leave the house?" They'd finished having the windows repaired yesterday, and things were finally shifting back to normal. Until the media had gotten wind that they'd returned.

"We should never have attempted to anchor ourselves to the human world," said MacLir.

"I will see to all arrangements," said Lucky. "The tunnels, or…" he trailed off uncertainly as the faces around him turned sour.

"I disagree," said Robin. "How can we fade back into legend when the Tua De are already out in the world? At least a hundred were placed in new homes in the human realm after the underground tunnels flooded."

"People know about us," agreed Clara, "they know what we can do. We aren't in the middle ages. No little towns with local legends. People have photos. We'll probably be in history books. It's too late for hiding."

"Well, I can't deal with this anymore," said Amy, waving her arms at the door, then over her head, before stomping to a chair and sinking into it with her arms folded.

"I can't have my family in danger," said MacLir quietly, looking at his hands. "So, maybe we don't go back to legend. Either way, we can't live here."

Piper watched the keys rattle on the keyring. Six of them, each in the colors of the rainbow. Red, orange, yellow, green, blue, purple. All so different, yet so alike. She'd lived with three Tuatha Dé Danann for a while now, and she couldn't tell the difference. Robin was a kind father, and Brigit was a caring healer. Lucky could get a little full of himself, but he had a good heart. Other than inborn magic, what was the difference between them? Nothing she could see. The beginnings of an idea were forming, the pieces assembling. She needed to step back to see the bigger picture.

"MacLir… what was the problem you were trying to solve this morning? I heard you talking to Lucky and Brigit about it."

"What do with the Tua De in the tunnels? Living conditions are terrible. A war with the humans was the worst way to try to fix it, but we don't see a good path forward either."

"I know they can't live above ground in the Otherworld realm, but is there a reason they can't live in the human realm?"

"Unless you are half-human, like me, it's against the law," pointed out Robin.

"The law… whose law?" asked Piper. The idea was swirling around in her head. She almost had it.

"The High Court," said Brigit.

"Is that the same High Court that was blown up by a bomb a couple weeks ago?" asked Piper.

Everyone in the room stilled as her point sunk in. "It would still be the law, even if the court is dead," said MacLir. "However, if the next court was willing, they could… change the law?"

Piper grinned. "If most of the fae flooded out of fairyland and merged with the humans, it would be a sensation. Then, we'd be old news. No knocking on our door. No newspaper headlines."

"It wouldn't stop," said Amy. "They would still pester us since no one else can hand out babies and creative breakthroughs like I can."

"We could train the fae to do the same magic as us—" Piper began.

Brigit shook her head, "They can't join the human world. It seems like the obvious easy fix, but where would they live? Where would they work?"

"We'll set up a business, train Tua De to take house calls," clarified Piper. "That would give them an income. Better yet, we'll train some of them to run their own businesses and hire each other. It will all run on human belief, yeah? So, we make them all gods. Give them stronger powers. Then give them work."

"Thrust into a high-tech world, without high school diplomas or citizenship, they might flounder," warned Robin.

"You did okay. They'll learn." Piper's mind buzzed with all things that would be put into place. It was an ambitious project, but she was sure it would work. She had a gut feeling about it and was learning to trust her gut more these days.

CHAPTER 23

Clara

Clara accepted a big bowl of mashed potatoes from Amy, dumped some on her plate, and passed it to Tamlin with a smile. "So," Clara said, "the news says you are the new High King."

Tamlin smiled back, "Only temporarily. I have more exciting things to do with my life than sitting around being a king." The boy glanced at his friend Sam as he said it, and they smiled.

"The headlines I saw said 'The Crowning of the Last High King of the Once Great Tuatha Dé Danann," said Brigit with a pleased chuckle. "Even though it's the end of an era, the footage of you being crowned on the Hill of Tara looked great."

"My goal is to follow Piper's plan. Get every last Tuatha Dé Danann out of the Otherworld, then I'll disband the ruling High Court and let everyone live as they please."

"A worthy goal!" shouted Lucky, pounding his ale mug on the table. The god of travelers already appeared a little tipsy. Clara had never seen him so happy.

A calm had settled into her own heart as the situation resolved. Finally, the war was truly over, the Tua De would have some peace, and she had a stable place to live out her days surrounded by people she loved.

"Did you decide what to do about immortality? And the nightly feast?" asked MacLir from the head of the table.

"Disbanded," said Tamlin. "Our last official feast was two nights ago, but almost no one was in attendance. So the jerky program is also dissolved. If my people join the humans permanently, we'll all be mortal together."

"I would think people would object to that," said Amy with a worried frown.

"We've been alive without truly living for long enough," said Brigit, rubbing her belly and smiling down at the new life growing inside her. "It's time to move on and grow old together." Lucky added his hand to hers and kissed her cheek.

"Many people believe the same," said Tamlin. "My generation will never have tasted immorality and don't want to." As they became more focused on the meal in front of them, all talking stopped, and the only sounds were the clinking of utensils.

Later, when the last of the dessert was gone, Piper spoke up for the first time all night. "You promised to tell us some history."

Tamlin smiled at her, his eyes sparkling. "Yes, I did. Do you have something specific you wanted to know?"

"Where did Fia come from? MacLir can't remember, and no one can tell me. Even Fia's explanation was confusing."

"As one of the highest ranking Tuatha Dé Danann in my clan, I was taught the history of my civilization through records stolen from Ireland's past High Court. They guarded their secrets well. Strong, powerful, and long-lived compared to humans, we are a nation of leaders. But too many leaders all vying for power can be a dangerous problem. The most violent clan started destructive wars and were banished for their crimes."

"See, banishing works," muttered Lucky to MacLir, who backed his head away from Lucky's breath.

"Not exactly," said Tamlin. "In this case, the burden was only passed on. The whole clan was ejected from our home realm in small ships. These specially designed ships were made like a slingshot. Propelled once, never to take off again. It's unclear in the histories how they were transported through realms, but Fia came with them. My ancestors landed in the human realm and immediately took up their old ways, causing trouble, and starting wars. Conquering the local inhabitants of Ireland."

"So, we did come from the sky," said Brigit. "I'd always wondered about that. I was sure it was mistranslated and just meant north."

"I guess I didn't notice when they came," said MacLir. "But I was young when it happened."

"You are even younger now," commented Lucky, poking his friend's arm.

MacLir cut his eyes to Lucky and playfully slapped his hand away, saying, "New body, old memories."

Piper laughed, but Clara decided it might be tinged with anxiety at what might have been, if they had not been able to locate the memories. MacLir leaned over and caught her face in his hands, stopping her nervous laugh with a reassuring kiss.

Hazel

The school bell rang loudly above Hazel's locker. It was a sound she had found enchanting days ago but was starting to annoy her. Taking a science book from the stack, she shoved it in her backpack and shut the locker.

"Hey girl!" The boppy little American using the locker next to her seemed tardy as often as Hazel. Either that, or she was intentionally following Hazel around. In fact, after getting their family's paperwork approved and settling here, everyone had been extra friendly to her at school and in the new neighborhood.

Pushing her way through the hallway, she grinned at the perfectly normal sight of so many teenagers chatting or using their lockers. Some showed off their magic to classmates. Not the only Tua De student sent to this town, she smiled at seeing magic in the human world.

Her mother was so happy to have her daughter back that she didn't hesitate when Hazel asked to move to America during the evacuation of the Otherworld. Countries worldwide happily accepted any magic user that agreed to do a certain amount of work for the government in exchange for citizenship. Her parents were training hard to fit into their new society, grandmama finally had a comfortable bed, and Hazel had a house within walking distance of a mall.

In Hazel's last class of the day, she watched the one person she desperately wanted as a friend, or maybe more than a friend. They had not spoken yet, and Hazel wondered if the girl knew who she was. Although, with all the fanfare at her arrival, she couldn't see how it was possible not to. It was Friday, and if she didn't talk to the girl today, she'd lose her chance and stress over it during the weekend.

As class wrapped up, she realized she had not heard a single word of it but figured she'd gone this long without school. What was a single hour comparatively? She smoothed her floral sundress, the best she had, worn today, in anticipation of finally officially meeting the girl in her science class. Pushing back her hair and shrugging on her backpack, ignoring the rising panic that made her sweat, Hazel rehearsed the eight words she wanted to say. However, when she braced and looked over, ready to casually make eye contact, the girl was darting out the classroom door ahead of her.

Hazel rushed to catch up but found no sign of her in the busy hallway. Shoulders drooping, she trudged to the outer door and kicked it open, ready to give up. Going through the doorway, she was bumped from behind.

"Oh, sorry," said a voice much too close to her ear.

Hazel glanced back and was face to face with the science-class-girl. All her previous anxiety rushed back into her stomach and brain. Feeling queasy, she blurted, "Want to go to the mall with me?"

"You're Hazel, right? The Irish girl." When Hazel nodded, the girl smiled and continued, "I'm new here too. I'd love to go to the mall with you."

They chatted as they walked, falling into conversation with ease. Her new friend looked nothing like Emma, but Hazel was already starting to feel the comfort of finding a kindred spirit. She and Emma had parted on good terms before she left, but Hazel realized that although they'd had fun together, they had nothing in common but shoplifting and overthrowing governments.

Hazel was ready to build a calm and prosperous life around her magical skills, something her mother never had the chance to do at her age. With the sun warming her skin and a new friend at her side, she finally felt hope for the future.

Piper

MacLir grabbed one edge of the blanket Piper was shaking out, and they laid it on the deck of Wave Sweeper. Setting Emily down on the blanket, MacLir stretched out on his back next to her. Emily promptly crawled away, adding to the calluses forming on her knees from her newfound skill in movement.

Vixen rushed to take up her position guarding the dip at the top of the rope ladder. "Thank you, Vixen," sent Piper, smiling at the dog who gave her such assistance keeping Emily safe.

"I'll always be here for you and Emily," Vixen assured her solemnly.

"I make no such promise," put in Flutter, jumping onto the bench and beginning a vigorous bath. "Maybe one day I'll switch to Lucky's house since at least he's willing to give me tuna every day."

"Only because he doesn't have to live with the smell after," sent Piper, sitting cross-legged next to MacLir, and putting his head in her lap.

The ship rocked gently in the waves just offshore as the wind picked up. She could make out lights coming on inside their big house up on the cliff, as the summer sun set in the west. "Wherever you are is my home, but I'm glad we're staying at the house."

"I'm glad too, for all of us. I was worried for a while," said MacLir.

"I know you were worried." She began playing with his hair, running fingers through it and twirling it around. She'd found it gave her something to do with her hands and relaxed them both.

"The Voiceless Pure is truly gone this time. Brigit and her team have been monitoring the Tua De out in the world, and everyone is settling nicely."

Piper nodded, but realized his eyes were closed, and said, "Good."

"I don't know how it could have gotten so out of hand. I'll be more active as a guardian in the Otherworld realm in the future. Maybe train Emily to learn some of the guardian duties one day."

Piper pictured a young Emily learning to wield water like MacLir. She'd already seen Emily in visions, so it was easy to imagine the two of them on a beach moving water with ease. Or maybe Emily would be able to talk to sea creatures? Perhaps she'd have none of MacLir's powers, which would be fine too.

MacLir's mind seemed to head in the same direction as hers, and he said, "Magic being out in the human world makes it safer for Emily to grow up, so she won't be seen as odd."

Any daughter of mine will probably always be seen as odd, thought Piper, but she hoped she was wrong. Maybe if the world could learn to appreciate magic users, they could also learn to accept other types of people.

"All the world's children will grow up with magic now," continued MacLir. "Seeing it or using it, I wonder what the new change in the world will bring for them?"

"Acceptance?" guessed Piper, still dreaming of a world that welcomed differences.

"That's a big grand goal, but one we should all aim for," agreed MacLir.

"I accept you. Just the way you are," said Piper, leaning down to kiss him softly.

"I love everything about you," MacLir told her, grasping her hand to give it a quick squeeze. "I'm so glad you stayed with me," he added, pulling her down to cuddle next to him.

"For forever," Piper reminded him, tucking her head into his shoulder.

Together they gazed up at the sliver of moon and bright stars visible above the last rays of sunset.

BIO

Starr Green is an autistic author living in the Pacific Northwest and has a degree specializing in Environmental Communication from Oregon State University. As a teen, she was delighted by all the worlds she discovered in the local library. Her debut novel Castaway Strangers was the first of her many fantasy books with female autistic characters.

Find out more at: starrgreeninfo.com

Books by Starr Green:

•

CASTAWAY STRANGERS

•

Wave Sweeper Trilogy
SAILING IN THE SKY
BELIEF IN THE REALM
TREASURE IN THE DEEP

•